Stillicide

Cynan Jones

GRANTA

Granta Publications, 12 Addison Avenue, London W11 4QR
First published in Great Britain by Granta Books, 2019
This paperback edition published by Granta Books, 2020

A CIP catalogue record is available from the British Library

9 8 7 6 5 4 3 2 1

ISBN 978 1 78378 709 8
eISBN 978 1 78378 562 9

www.granta.com

Text designed by Lindsay Nash
Typeset in Vendome by Avon DataSet Ltd, Arden Court, Alcester,
Warwickshire B49 6HN
Printed and bound by CPI Group (UK) Ltd, Croydon, CR0 4YY

For P.F. and J.F.

stillicide, n
ˈstɪlɪsʌɪd

1. *A continual dropping of water.*
2. Law – *A right or duty relating to the collection of water from or onto adjacent land.*

From Latin *stillicidium,* from *stilla* drop + *-cidium,* from *cadere* to fall.

CONTENTS

The Water Train

The boy's hand opened and closed as if he reached for a glass of water but it was just the nerves dying through his body.

With the thick rain the blood from the wound ran a thin washed pink.

Nearby again a pheasant crowed, a klaxon call as they make before thunder.

The bullet had gone in at the boy's jaw and removed that side.

Branner stood over the body, the rain hitting his hood, drumming out the last rush of the train. Heavy and rhythmic, heavy and rhythmic.

Felt the shudder drop from the ground as the train gained distance.

Still the boy's hand gaped, a fish dying in the air.

The rain hit Branner's hood. Hit. Hood. Made a shelter for his mind. A building he hadn't stepped out of yet. It closed him off.

The uppermost side of the boy's face was visible and perfect and untouched by the bullet.

Branner wore the earpiece out so he could hear the rain and the sergeant's voice seemed to come from afar.

– It was a kid, Branner said at the mic.

*

There is the silence as of after a great push of wind.

They stand at the crest of the field, overlook the ocean, the pines that stand in their line of sight.

She tightens her grip when she feels his words start.

– I don't want there to be pain.

Her hand tightens. Do not speak.

2

He wants to say, I do not want there to be time, to think of you in pain.

– I do not want time to think of you in pain.

The light intensifies, as if it grows in volume. Time. There is no movement to the air, but in the ground now a minute growing shake.

Then far in the distance the sea at the horizon seems suddenly to smooth, the way soft butter goes with the pass of a blunt knife.

She squeezes his hand, as if she silences the earth. Silences him.

I thought I would be stronger than this. Not this, not anger.

He is aware in the last seconds of her great dignified fear as the trees ahead of them explode. Explode with silence.

A bird crosses the sky. Lone and black. Burns mid-air, disintegrates to ash.

A split second before he wakes, the force comes through his eyes.

The dream is like a dry mouth.

The hiss in his earpiece brought Branner round, and he saw the red dot flash on the grid scanner in his hand. He was sheltered from the rain partially, pushed in against the willow at the fifty-metre line. The rain came down heavily. Subdued the dawn light.

The distraction was a relief. When he'd heard the doctor's words, they seemed spoken through water. Had grown every moment since in volume and solidity. Seemed now to knock against the shell of the dream he's had for weeks. A recurrence he braces for in sleep. The dream now like a premonition.

'I've seen it,' Branner said into his mic.

He watched the red dot shift across the scanner, hesitate, then apparently settle. A slight condensation come to the edges of the screen.

There was no way of knowing what the red dot was, but it was in the sector and big enough to trigger the sensors.

Deer. Dog. Man. If it was still alive and present when the water load passed, the defence guns of the train would fire automatically.

They weren't taking any chances now. Attacks on the line had increased.

Branner had the choice to stay out of the way or neutralise the risk himself. He could take the shot, or, if he could identify it as nothing threatening, call it in to the tower and they could stand the train guns down.

'Can you get there?' The sergeant's voice came through the earpiece, through the snap of rain on Branner's hood.

'I can get there,' Branner replied. It was relatively close. The opposite side of the track.

'Let the train guns take it,' said the sergeant.

Branner felt the old scar on his jaw catch slightly against the nap inside his hood.

'No. I'll go.'

It will be an animal, Branner thought. There's no need for it to pointlessly die.

The drops gathered and fell heavily from the long leaves of willow.

Branner checked his rifle and walked into the rain.

~

There was a slowness in the watch post. The rain patting on the corrugated roof.

The sergeant and the line officer watched Branner on the monitor – a green dot – zoomed in a few clicks. It was difficult for them to see only the green dot and not in their minds Branner himself.

Knowing about Branner's wife made them think of him differently.

'Where's the train?' The voice that broke abruptly into the room seemed to have no connection to the dot.

'On time. Forty seconds to sector.' The digits flicking.

The rain thickened, drumming the watch post. Thumping down.

'Don't you love summer?' the sergeant said.

'They should have built a gutter to the city,' said the officer. 'This rain. Not a train track.'

'Well, *we* won't run out.'

The sergeant felt the warmth of the coffee through the cup, mesmerised for a moment by the swirls on the surface of the liquid. The contained clatter of the runnelled rain.

The hostile red dot did not move away. It moved just sporadically in the same place.

'It's waiting,' the sergeant guessed. Tried to sense something from the dot.

It was a dog last night, caught up in the bramble. Scruffy, thick-set mongrel thing.

'Is the growth there cleared?' he asked the line officer.

'Eighteen months ago.'

Branner was leaving it late to get over the track. Why was he doing that?

A barely perceptible tremor started in the water that hung in the rain collector just outside. The sergeant looked for the tremor in his coffee cup.

'They should just burn it away every year,' he said.

He could never take his eyes from the counter in the last few seconds. The digits fluttering. Damn, he's leaving it late.

They knew it was coming but their bodies tensed when the tone came on.

'Okay,' the sergeant said, into the comms. 'Train in sector. You need to speed it up, John.'

~

Branner went over the track by one of the old footings of the pipeline that had taken water to the city before the train.

The memory thudded against the shell the dream made around his mind, a dull moth against bright glass. The time they met. Out here as a young soldier on patrol, before he transferred to the police. An activist group had bombed the pipe. He'd been one of the few still standing. Dragged drowning men from the spilled water.

She was with the medic team. He was the first person she had ever sewn up.

The rain had brought the biting insects out and they hung above the line in brief clouds, hypnotised by the high-pitched hum feeding back from the pressure converters.

There was a smell of wet metal and stone.

Branner was not connected properly to himself. He could not step out of the moment with her in his dream just before the trees exploded.

It was a muntjac we were eating, that day, he thought. Before the charge went off. It's probably a muntjac, this red dot.

As he went over the track, he paused to put his hand on the rail, his habit to touch the world to try to bring it back. But he could not fully focus.

He saw himself for a split second reflected in the rain collected on the solar sleeper. *A black bird bursting into ash.*

Dissipated into sky, as the rain broke his brief image.

Not too distantly a pheasant called, shuttered its wings, sensing the coming shudder in the air.

~

At the watch post, the blackbirds started to call and quickly their noise was thorough. The rain collector now trembled where it hung, and the post hummed with the bizarre accidental song that came into its iron stays.

'Why isn't he there?' the sergeant asked. At least the green dot had gained pace. For a while it had seemed to falter, as if the dot itself had to cut its way through the dark backdrop of the monitor screen.

They saw Branner when he came into the cameras, as he went over the track.

'Can you make this?' the sergeant asked, bluntly into the comms.

They saw Branner, the rain somehow haloed around him, as if he moved in a bubble.

'I can.' But the voice was far off.

'He's leaving it late, Sarge.'

'It's Branner,' said the sergeant. 'He'll shoot.'

The rain intensified again. A noise oncoming. The train transporting ten million gallons of water to the city at two hundred miles per hour.

Don't go red, John, the sergeant thought. You're not the type. You told us you were fine.

All he'd have to do is switch off his greenlighter and . . .

The digits fluttering, the rain collector swinging now.

'Just leave it, Branner. Stay clear. It'll be another dog.'

~

The rain hit with the rhythm of train wheels. Hit hood. Hit his hood. His brain was in a cave.

'What is it?' asked the sergeant.

'I do not know.'

There was just the red dot, anonymous, a threat, superimposed on the undergrowth in the mid-scope of Branner's rifle, moving sometimes minutely.

11

'We cannot greenlight it without a visual, Branner. Take the shot,' the sergeant ordered.

Branner could feel the train now in the ground. The shudder come, a growing shake, still the veil of dream, the image of the pine trees bursting. *Explode. Explode with silence.*

He thought desperately of his wife.

A shudder through the earth, his body.

The future now, a drop from a high building.

I do not want there to be time, to think of you in pain.

I could just switch off my greenlighter. That's all it would take. The train guns wouldn't recognise me. And they'd fire.

He imagined for a moment the thrashed material lifted in suspension in the air, a cloud of smashed greenery and blitzed stick, the thick earth orbiting through the pink miasma of his own obliterated cells. The sudden leap of everything, before settling down to ground.

He felt drips riddle down the body of the gun and well against his hands.

His soul was just there, curled up in the scope, as if he could witness it.

Hit. Hood. The rain. The train. The puddles gathered round him where he knelt vibrating, loosening. Ten million gallons of water, two hundred miles an hour.

'Branner.'

There was urgency now in the sergeant's voice, the rain, the air seeming to shatter ahead of the oncoming force.

Branner thought of the crossfire shatter clatter; the stub guns rippling like a millipede's legs.

A great noise. Then I would be gone. I wouldn't have to live with it. The doctor's words.

He felt the rifle calculate for distance, calculate for force.

'. . . seconds,' lost in the thickening noise. The bullet's path, a dream burst into flame and char, disintegrate to ash. The train some crashing wave.

It would happen with no more effort than it took to pick away a hangnail.

'Clearing sector,' Branner said.

It's all you have now. Duty.

Paper Flowers

The electric passenger trains hiss along the nearby tracks and it sounds like I remember wind does, moving through wide forests. A rhythm to it, a pulse almost, as if the city's breathing.

There is only early morning light. Then the Water Train passes. Different. A weight of sound. The sound of a great waterfall crashing into a pool. It has the power church bells must used to have.

I have seen it pass above the houses on its lifted steel tracks and felt the shake it brings to the floor. Seen its hoses and pipes. The heavy protection.

It is meant to look magnificent, impregnable, but it looks uncertain, like a person others have decided to make into their hero.

It's always about the image of a thing, in most minds.

It thunders by. And after it has passed, all the sounds seem to drop from the air for a moment. As if it leaves a vacuum.

I hear the soilmen then come for the soilets, clattering in the street below. Nita moves gently, next to me in the bed, the faint acidity of alcowash and the covering scent in her hair, and I am certain the noise they make will wake her.

There is something daring about the way they make such noise. As if to provoke you to complain, so they can say 'Is this a job you'd like to do? Is this a job you'd like us *not* to do?' The games we make of our jobs.

But she stays asleep.

Hillie though, her daughter, wakes. I hear her get up from her mattress and quietly play behind the sheet they modestly hang across the bedsit when I come here. 'Happy in her own skin.' A phrase I learnt from Nita when we met. Like an object she gave me to keep.

I hear the little one say 'pooh' and 'yuk', the stink now as they empty the chute bins out into the truck. Lie there, listening to the soilmen move along the buildings, the throb of the pipe sucking, chugging up the fibre and muck until they are too far down the street to hear; but the smell lingers. Treacly. Or perhaps just seems so, because my mouth is sticky and dry. The cement dust gets everywhere.

That first time I saw them, they were sitting together with their legs through the railings, looking out over the edge of the embankment, above the drained riverbed, pretending to be on a ship. They were pretending the city was a great old-fashioned ocean liner sailing through the sea.

The next day, after shift, I went to the same spot. To rest my eyes after the glare of the Dock. I hadn't been able to stop thinking about the great ocean ship. Had lain awake. Travelling myself to the countries of the world. To home.

But this time there she was, crouched intently, trying – I thought at first – to fish a thorn out of her thumb.

Until she leant back, and I saw she had conjured a paper rose in her hand.

I hadn't noticed the first time, but there were flowers laid on a blanket, nearby. Hillie was going to and fro to the dry riverbank, bringing rubbish for her mother to use.

I had wanted to hear her describe again the world go by from the deck of a ship. But instead she had a little fire going in a rusted can, and she melted an ancient plastic bottle to use as drops of glue.

Instead of make-believing the big wide world, here she was. Building flowers.

I couldn't take my eyes off her. I thought I was over that sort of thing.

I smell the krill blocks from supper at the end of the room. Hear the toing and froing of the passenger trains. Stare at the paint peeling from the ceiling, the curling flakes. Like turning pages.

Let time go a little.

But I begin to feel in my body I should look at the clock. Just thinking of the polishers makes my shoulder blades ache. My hands sore.

But perhaps the protest will stop the work today. They say half a million people will be on the march. It's not that many, I suppose, in the context of the city. And few of them will be people who are actually affected.

But the Mayor has announced that far more families will be moved from their homes than the water company first said.

Two years since the project started. An anniversary today. Of the beginning of construction, that started with a ribbon of buildings being demolished, before we could begin. A gash cut through the city to steer the iceberg through.

How often the process of construction starts with destruction.

Now they say the run-off channels need a wider margin than they thought. The stillicide channels along the tow-track to the Dock, to catch the melting ice water.

More homes will be knocked down. More families will be moved.

And we'll be one of them. Well. Nita and Hillie. They are the 'they' who will be moved. This bedsit.

But, she says, we might get somewhere better. Nearer to the riverbed. Maybe with a view.

Somewhere up high, I say. Like a bird.

Somewhere where we will not hear the soilmen. Or be rattled by the trains.

We'll wait and see.

I reach onto the floor and pop out an immunotab, crunch it in my dry mouth. I should get up and spray myself with alcowash, take a tooth lozenge then boil up some of the sterilised grey water for tea.

I know though, once I rise Nita will wake, the rhythm will take over.

'What will you do today?' I'll ask. And she will say 'I'll ride the train to the riverbank. Like every day. And there I will make flowers. And then I will go to *sell* my flowers, at the foot of the busy bridge.' And she will then say, as she always says, 'Will you be with us later?'

I close my eyes. A few more moments here. My body already moving towards the day's work. The whine of the polisher. The dust, like flour. Making paste round the seal of my eyeguard.

The way the heat throws itself back off the walls.

I think of all the water locked up in the cement of the Dock. One hundred and fifty litres bound up in each cubic metre of concrete. They do not talk about that.

And how much of that becomes powder in the air.

Nita moves. Stretches, and the tattoo of a bird seems to dip along the tan sky of her skin.

On the table close to the bed, the bare light catches her scissors and thread.

An old lump of smoky white glass, long-ago long-smoothed by the river. It looks like a chunk of impossible ice.

I try to imagine the berg again, there in the Dock. When finally we've finished.

I can't help but be in awe.

Millions in this city. The Thames tanks just can't hold enough, Water Train or not.

However many little watercourses they find and reopen. Like the one they've found that runs beneath the Dock site.

Think of it. The city was full of streams and rivers, centuries ago. But they covered them with tunnels and built houses over them.

And now we have this. An iceberg!

People are astonishing.

My father used to say, 'We fear the worst and do our best.'

We have the imagination and the science to tow an iceberg into the centre of a city.

Hillie comes quietly through and climbs onto the bed, as she does every morning, like a little person-clock.

I pretend to be asleep. Sense she puts her finger on her mother's bird tattoo.

Then, from the street there is a sudden cheer. A hiss. A pile of voices. A crisp shatter against the window glass.

The little one looks up, as startled as I am, and I make a shush with my finger and mouth. Then I lift her off the bed, Nita uncurling.

I make a funny face to Hillie, squeeze it up at the risk of waking her mother, the little one wide-eyed with wonder; and carry her the few steps to the window, shift the curtain to one side.

Kids have hacked the old water main – I just catch sight of them, running, their bright clothes flashing like deers' tails – and for a moment the leftover pressure pushes out the residual water, in a spray like a fountain. Catching rainbows of early morning light.

Hillie is a contained squeal of delight.

Laughter in the alley.

The dirt at the side of the street so dry it pushes the water away.

The pressure abating. Runnels of water thickly down the glass. 'Stillicide'.

And the little one watches.

The street has changed colour. Birds have come to drink already. Sparrows and pigeons, as if from nowhere.

Hillie winds her hand in my hair, the way she does, teasing it into stiff clumps. In her other hand, the soft toy she is currently in love with that her mother made from scraps. She watches the street, mesmerised.

Winding my hair like my own children did.

Enjoying how different my hair is from Nita's.

Even with the extra water tokens that we have as part of our pay, us workers, it's impossible to wash our hair properly.

We let the dust thicken in it and make joke hairstyles. Mad, crazy hairstyles that we can tell each other by. With the eyeguards and the work clothes and blankets of dust we otherwise all look the same.

'When we're done with the polishers, we'll shave our heads,' we say. A thing that makes the little one wriggle happily with horror.

'We'll have some party,' we say. 'We'll swim in the stillicide channels.' In the meantime, let's look like pirates.

All the ways the world has changed and pirates still are pirates!

Nita joins us at the window. I did not hear her rise and that makes me feel that for a moment I've been absent.

I've been thinking about swimming. My whole body in deep water.

I should take them to the beach . . .

Hillie points to the street and sways slightly as she's kissed. I think of my own children, home, the scent of their crowns. Before I travelled here for work. The dream that they would join me. How fast the years have passed.

But.

Nita puts her arm around me; pigeons clatter from the street. One seems more a dove amongst them. Seems to carry a coppery metallic sheen, like a beetle's wing.

A scruffy dog trots up and puts its nose in the water. A boy, just as scruffy, trots behind.

'Would you like tea?' I ask Nita. Feel her nod. As if she gives permission for the day to begin.

'What will you do today?' I ask. And she says, 'We'll ride the train to the dried-up river. Like we do every day.'

And every time she says it, I remember how we met. Sailing on a make-believe liner around a make-believe world.

They will make flowers, then go to the bridge.

And while I stand there, white-faced, in the beating heat of concrete, my arms rattling in their sockets with the work, I will imagine them. My Naiads washed up.

I will hear, through the roar of the work, the snip of their scissors.

I will imagine them filling the city with blooms. Dancing over the streets. Planting flowers in the cracks of the kerbs.

BUTTERFLIES

Ruth steps into the pool of warmth ebbing off the tarmac between the beautiful ornate old gates and the high fence that blocks the park from view.

Already, the sounds of the city seem muffled. Stripped of urgency and flattened.

She has a little flush of nerves when she fears she might have left the ticket in her coat back at the staff room in the hospital. But no. It's there. An old-fashioned paper slip, a thank you from a patient's family.

The original railings – tipped like arrowheads, all around the grounds – are finished with black paint. She can't help but think the paint is somehow melted in the sun. It looks still wet and makes her want to touch it. Recalls the hard liquorice she used to covet from her father as a child, small diamonds sticky in her mouth; the way she and her brother Leo used to see which of them could keep one longest on their tongue.

~

There's a booth with an actual person, wearing a name badge. So surprising it makes her childish. But then, there's a warm nervousness just beneath her skin right now. Ever since she lied to Colin. Told him she would be on a late shift and said yes to tonight.

There's been nothing recently. And every time she thinks about it, she recognises just how long she means when she says 'recently'.

His mind is always somewhere else. Always with the same excuse, 'It's work.'

This business with the Ice Dock. He's certain there's some big scandal to uncover. But when is he not? Certain this is his chance to write his breakthrough story. Always, she thinks, something is the chance to write his breakthrough story.

He's sure other journalists are safe in someone's pocket.

This piece. The cycling. His love of antique letter openers. He has obsessions. Colin.

She's realised that's all she was to him, and that for a few years now, she's been little more than furniture.

That for a long, long time, every time she goes home, she hopes he will be different. Will have lifted from his bubble.

He was still up when she came in from her actual late shift last night on the ward.

His finger pattering away at his tablet, the way someone would poke another person in the chest if they were angry.

Don't get cold, she'd said to him. And he'd said, 'Do you mean emotionally?' Not even looking up.

Always so clever with his words.

~

Ruth shows the ticket and is let through an old-fashioned turnstile. It clicks and snaps ingeniously. The bar rotates into her bum. A cheeky bump of encouragement. 'It's okay . . .' Into a different world.

A group of young mothers sit on the grass. Their children bright as flowers.

Couples walk on the paths. Blackbirds toy in the leaf litter, flick up the ornamental bark.

Ruth has never looked up and seen so few people outdoors in this city. Feels a strange sense of vertigo at the unbusyness, the space. A nostalgia for the beach she grew up next to.

Remembers watching Leo learn to walk in their parents' garden by the sea.

~

She builds up the courage to sit. The give of the ground ever-so-slight. Firm and warm. Rests her hand into the soft nap of grass, uncertain that she should.

It takes her a while to realise the hum is not the city traffic but the sound of insects. Tiny flies displaying, staying in one place in the air.

The lawn is littered with clover. Another plant she does not know. Tiny. A crowd of heart-shaped leaves with tight-grouped yellow flowers that look like knots in thread.

There's a gentle breeze. That she *hears* more than feels. That knocks the nearby leaves a little.

Odd-looking alginate bags hang amongst the trees and shrubs, like funny plastic fruit. With the opaque haze of the soundproof pods around the patients' beds. Leaves bunched up, the bags tied tightly at the neck with string.

She assumes the plants have some sort of infection.

Notices each type of leaf makes a sound all of its own. The rattle of dried peas in a child's toy; the shush sound in a shell. Respirators. Laboured breath.

She pushes the thought of the ward away.

. . . Breathlessness . . .

Tonight. Maybe.

A tickle on her skin.

~

She watches an aphid stumble through the faint blonde hairs of her arm; its curious feelers flittering busily, tasting the paths of her salt.

31

For a moment she is lost, imagining how the world must look through eyes so small.

Finds the thought of it impossible. That it carries its machinery packed up inside. Its intestines and nervous wires, its breathing apparatus. Something so minute.

Its tiny eyes are perfect. Absolutely pin-prick black.

~

All around the park, bushes and trees are carefully spaced, or clustered into a balanced fringe. The songs of birds. Movements, every so often, a prattle in the branches.

She walks. Feels sun on her shoulders; a warmth tracing her edges. Reminds her of her shape.

A buttercup bends with the ballast of a bumblebee; a bluebottle iridescent, like a blue piece of glass.

Beetles, like articles of cast-off jewellery, scuttle in the grass.

She takes some sips from her shift ration, holding the water in the funny space under her tongue.

Last time she saw a bumblebee she caught it in a cup. Rescued it from the fake daisies pattern of the staff room tablecloth.

It kept trying to come back in, after she had set it free, bumping on the window.

~

In the glasshouses the heat is stifling and rich. The lights are open in the roof, but she is sure that if she wished she could part the air with her hands.

The shock of a cactus flower. A bright cerise pink.

She rolls the names of labelled plants round on her tongue, the way she does with chemicals. Coloured pills in paper cups.

Gymnocalycium mihanovichii.

Astrophytum capricorne.

Delosperma cooperi.

Not knowing whether or not she speaks the Latin properly.

You don't know unless you're told, she thinks.

You don't know unless you try it . . .

A cactus stands taller than herself, skeletal and branching. *Naked with your arms up in the air . . .*

Succulent.

The word feels succulent itself.

This cactus, says a sign, can store a tonne of water fully grown.

When she sees the insect-eating plants, the sticky drops on some of them make her purse her lips.

~

In the orchid house, as if hair clips have been used, there are plants held on branches with thin wires. A sense of moisture in the air.

The flowers bold and blatant. Vivid. Seem fake. The paper flowers on the patients' tables more real-seeming than these.

Loosed and partly sunken in the soft moss bed, a gorgeously puckered bloom.

She feels a rush, a heady indecision as she softly tunnels her finger to it. The confident intricacy it has. Her blue uniform reflected in the glass of a display case. The sense she steps towards herself.

She's still thinking of the cactus flower. It's daring garishness. What underwear she should put on tonight.

As she leaves the room she sees the plaque. The collection sponsored by the media company that owns the newspaper Colin works for.

And it's as if he's seen her. As if she has been caught.

~

Seeing the name of Colin's company has invaded. Told her somehow that he knows. That brings her don't-be-silly voice again.

'You can't.'

The soft electric recklessness that's set in beneath her skin seems suddenly chased away. A hollow left.

A slight sick feeling.

The liquorice, always in the end, disappearing on her tongue.

~

She sits outside the Grand Pavilion at a white table on a patio, before a meadow of longer grass.

Impossibly, the grasses dance with small blue butterflies, the pale blue of her uniform. Others with buff-coloured wings, fringed, some of them, with orange. Some petal-shaped white flags. Then comes a sudden scratch of grasshopper song. And the buzz of honey bees.

The cells of her body seem to understand that this is how things should be.

How things *could* be. A money spider on her pale skin.

Her body adrift on Colin's huge indifference.

There's something about the way the butterflies flit above the grass that reminds her how the ward lights catch the translucent covers round the beds. The way their blue uniforms float in the corner of their eye, reflect briefly as they pass.

From the inside, it must seem as if you're looking out from a cocoon. The thin skin of a chrysalis.

Hoping for change. Waiting. Hoping that you will find a way to emerge from your own old skin, to the idea you have of yourself renewed.

She looks up. Lets the coffee fill her mouth and holds it for a while. Feels it re-warm as she does.

She almost wants Colin now to know. To watch her. To have him see her do it. And when she thinks of that, his eyes on her tonight, a warm edge comes back to her skin.

That was always a difference between her brother and her. Leo would just chew the liquorice. Could never wait.

But she. She was always so careful. As if not giving in to that temptation made her somehow better. And all the while the thing was just dissolving anyway.

She'd always put it down to a boy girl thing, but now she wasn't so sure.

Maybe Leo was right. What's the point of having a thing just to see if you can keep it?

~

She had decided that the alginate bags amongst the trees and shrubs protected gangs of caterpillars from predatory birds. That the bags were hatching butterflies. But the bright kid behind the cafe counter explained, pointing at the mural.

The strange bags in amongst the leaves were hung there to collect water. It's amazing, what we do.

'Leaves breathe out,' he said. 'There's water in their breath. After a while they breathe enough to make a single coffee.'

She does not care how much it costs.

Yes, she thinks. Tonight. I will. In knickers the colour of the cactus flower.

Wonders if the taste of coffee will stay there on her lips.

A dizziness from the thought coming, that it will be so new, to feel a body that is so nearly like her own.

COAST

David gave an abrupt flick with the handle of the knife and the limpet prattled off the piling.

Many times he'd done this, but each time felt the mixed sensation of apology and surprise at the morbid, expressive putty of creature set into the shell.

It did not look appetising and was not; but 'I am an old man,' David joked to himself. 'They are plentiful, and I neither have to run, nor – which I'd surely have to were I fishing – pray.'

He felt, every time, the further surprise, newly, at how a thing that had taken on such ancientness to look at from outside was so bright within.

The pad of his thumb around the smooth inside; the coarse surface on his fingertip. Of all the artefacts he and his wife had collected from the beach he'd take a limpet shell for wonder.

The day seemed indecisive. The breakers of the outgoing tide smushed and drew. Sand martins spun from their tunnels in the cliffs.

Every so often there was a ticking pitter-patter as the low breeze rattled the dry seaweed.

There had been another August storm.

It had washed the sand from the foundations and fallen rubble of two houses that had recently gone onto the beach, and from the skeletal groyne that stretched into the sea.

Against the shifting contours of the shore, the pilings of the old sea defences looked ancient and immoveable. Pitted and barnacled and hung with algae.

David considered that the principles, of how to build a structure to hold back waves, were the same principles his team had used to build footings for the pipeline, all those years ago. Before they had a train to carry water to the city.

That had been his life. The engineering of support. Holding things back. Or holding things up. His wife, Helen, joked he should have designed bras.

He took a few more limpets. Where they were gathered into a family circle on the pilings, he could not take them. He never could. But he was even more conscious now of how it must be for one of a loving group to be knocked off the rock.

That was the hardest thing. Trying not to think of them, *his* family circle.

At least for the limpet everything seemed fine until that sudden tap from nowhere.

He stood and helped himself to a small diamond of liquorice from the tin he carried. The flavour sat well with the salt air.

He was patient with the stiffness in his back, knowing it would loosen as he walked.

The bright collecting bag was full enough. Helen was right. More sensible to use the gaudy colours now their eyes were going. He'd conceded this the third time he'd lost his grey canvas sack against the stones.

'You don't need camouflage for limpets.' She had a point.

As he headed off the beach, David stopped to watch the sand martins stall and speed along the brow of the collapsing grey cliff.

He had been amongst those who had torn down the nets the council put up some years ago to stop the birds nesting. Contributing to erosion, so they claimed! There was a whole ocean to hold back, but they opted to stop the half-ounce birds.

How long ago was that, he asked himself. Thirty something years? I was Leo's age, back then.

David came up what the sea had left of the steps. The tidal defence panels to either side were bleached grey, had the compact, matted look he imagined the pelt of a seal must have. That they were moulded from re-formed blades of decommissioned wind turbines seemed right.

First, he thought, a myopic attempt to harness Nature, now a hopeful bid to hold her back. Let's see how that goes.

Some things you can stop, he thought, other things you can't.

He turned a final time to nod to the beach. Remains of other buildings showed strewn through the sand. And as he looked out over the flat sea, he saw the flash at the horizon. The limpets clickety-clacked as he set down the bag and unbuttoned his pocket for the binoculars.

'Well, look at that,' he said out loud. He'd seen the bergs go by a few times now, and every time felt the same gentle shock as seeing the inside of a shell.

There on the horizon, a trio of tiny boats, and behind them, towed, an iceberg,

Of all the things, he thought. They must have brought that through the storm.

He'd promised himself he'd go and see the Dock a few hours up the coast but hadn't yet. Wouldn't now. Instead he'd traded in the promise. Don't let this thing get the better of you until you see the giant city berg go by, when finally it does. Imagine the size that one will be! They'll need a fleet of tugs . . .

There is a magnificence to the idea, he thinks. They're breaking from the ice cap anyway. Why let them melt into the sea?

Like limpets, they're a ready crop. With a bit of effort.

David emptied the bright bag into the dry old sink and turned off the radio. Helen did not like quiet. At least, did not like quiet when she was alone in the house.

If he'd been out, he could follow her through the rooms she'd been in, clicking off the radios the same way they used to follow the kids as toddlers, picking up the toys they'd dropped. He chided her fondly.

Decades ago he'd brought her music, on Compact Discs. Something you could actually hold, give. 'It's not the same,' she'd said. 'It makes me have to choose what I want to listen to. Anyway. It's the talking. I like the talking.' She was fine with quiet when he was there.

That was another thing he made himself not think about. In the tougher moments he imagined her rattling about the empty house like a wooden ball. Taking a radio to bed.

*

'Leo!' His son was early. 'Look at you!'

David scratched the paddle of driftwood round the inside of the desalinator, cleaning the evaporation chamber.

'How's the beach?' asked Leo.

'I saw another iceberg!'

*

'I've near forgotten how to cook them,' Helen said, looking at the lamb chops.

'From the new-farm,' Leo said.

'Just because you didn't want to eat our limpets!'

Leo smiled.

'It's good to have it. Sheep. Milking cows. And they gave us chickens to look after ourselves.'

'Chickens!'

Leo smiled again.

'Our group of accommopods,' he said. 'We have a veg patch too.'

'You'll be running black market lamb chops up and down the country soon. No more of this bland stuff those superfarms grow. In the city's soil.'

David looked at his son. A cohesion had come to him. When he'd left a few years past for work at the reservoir there'd been a jerkiness about him. A need to go. Always a mechanic, this one. Ruth, on the other hand, was a carer from the start. Had more time for living things.

It was no surprise when Leo took a job with the Water Train. The scale of the thing, the awesomeness of transporting that much water; the science of it! Leo looked strong, like he was stepping towards a life he understood.

'And, you didn't bring Cora! Afraid I'll steal her from you? How did a grease monkey like you pull a woman with her brains? What is it that she does, again?'

'She's a thermo-fluctuationist.'

'What's a thermo-fluctuationist?'

'What's a grease monkey?'

'I guess I'll just grill them,' Helen said, staring at the chops.

*

Having got used to living without red meat, the smell of the cooking lamb brought on a temporary insanity. David had to stand outside.

The windowsills were heavy with lumps of rock and fossils. The strange curl of an ammonite.

'So you're not going to move?' said Leo.

Most people had opted to take the government relocation money.

'Careful what you wish for. These lamb chops. You might find us bunking in with you.'

'Dad,' said Leo patiently.

David looked at the bleached log of driftwood riddled with shipworm, the tunnelled shells embedded in the wood. He and Leo had carried it up from the beach last time he was here.

'Can non-workers move in?' asked David.

'Family, yes. In certain circumstances.'

David found he had to turn away from Leo then. He hadn't been able to imagine Helen having to stay with Ruth, as Ruth would want. Couldn't imagine her happy in the city. With Leo, she'd have space, and scale. And chickens, he tried to cheer himself.

The sun had not come out as it had threatened it might earlier, but a pleasant wind blew across the land bringing an earthy, wheaten smell that made the sea seem further away than it was.

'I've watched the sun rise over this beach all my life,' David said. 'Why would we move, now?'

'So you don't drown in your beds,' said Leo.

'It's fifteen, twenty years away. We won't be here for that.'

'One big storm, Dad.'

He looked at Leo gently. Leo was looking out over the hundred or so metres of grassland to the far-out tide and the remains of the buildings on the shore.

'They're like the sunken farmhouse we can see. When the reservoir is very low,' Leo said. 'Like now.'

'Tell me. While your mother's busy. These attacks?'

'We're fine. It's weird to see the guards. But we've not had any trouble. It's down the line the attacks are happening, really.'

'Like on the pipeline, early days,' David remembered.

'Your footings are still there, you know.'

'Built to stay.'

David's engineering sense was in his brain, his son's in his hands.

'Do they know,' David asked, 'who? Is making the attacks.'

'Angry people,' Leo said. 'No one properly organised. They don't think. Yet. They should go for the dam if they had any sense.'

*

Leo reached out to the bowl of salt, put some directly on his tongue. 'Do you hear it, from here? The Water Train?'

'Don't be duzzy,' Helen said.

David put down the stripped chop.

'I fancy we do sometimes, with the sea calm and the wind in the right direction. Now we don't have to shut our ears against the bloody turbines.'

The air had unfilled when they shut down the wind farm out on the sandbanks, the horrible whine dropping from the sky around the ocean.

They had not realised how much they had come to brace themselves against the sound until it was suddenly gone. The same had happened when the air traffic more or less stopped.

'Tell me,' David said, 'have you heard from your sister?'

'I'll see her soon,' Leo said. 'We're going to the city for the weekend, when the shifts work out. Cora and Ruth get on. We'll try and time it so Colin is away.'

'You're not a fan?'

'I can't believe she's with him still.'

Leo had balanced a pyramid crystal of salt on the tip of his upraised finger and it caught in the light of the window behind him with the brightness the iceberg had held on the sea.

'What did we do wrong, to raise a child who moves into the city?'

'You fed them limpets,' Leo said.

*

'Give Cora this.' David passed Leo the brooch.

'Dad!'

'Bronze Age, we think.' It was beautiful. It seemed to throb despite the dullness of the metal.

They found more and more things now, now the rising sea chewed away more broadly at the low clay coast.

'Take it,' he repeated to his son.

The nod his wife gave was almost imperceptible. As if she had heard him say, 'We can't take things with us, after all. Can we?'

Leo seemed to sense something extra from the brooch. Seemed about to speak.

But, 'Did you hear the old bandstand has gone into the ocean?' David cut off whatever it was Leo might have been about to say, indicating out to the peninsula, past the fishing boats rotting away upturned.

'And you used to be able to walk all the way to Holland from here,' he noted toyfully. 'Do you want to take some limpets back with you? Better than that lamb . . .'

Leo still seemed to be communicating somehow with the brooch.

'You know, they barely move more than half a metre from their home scar all their lives. They have a home scar. Chisel a little place out, limpets, on their rock.'

'So you tell me every time,' said Leo, patiently.

The sand martins were flicking by as the evening fell.

'We used to dance in that bandstand. Before you were born. Your mother and I.'

*

David stood by the desalinator. There had been little sun all day and the water sat murky in the sea tank. Hardly any had worked through into the collecting vat. The dust of the previously scraped-off salt rainbowed a little in the evaporation chamber as the sun dropped.

He sensed Helen near. Did not take his eyes from the white dome, promising himself.

Don't let it get the better of you. Not until the city berg's gone by . . .

He imagined the extraordinary sight. A fleet of tugs fanned across the water, a giant chunk of ice.

'You should have told him,' Helen said.

There was the endless, comforting sea. He took her hand. Her nails still as smooth as the inside of a shell. Her old skin.

'Then he'll just wait,' he said. 'Won't a shock be easier?'

CHAFFINCH

Tap tap. Tap tap.

There's a bird. Repeatedly. Beating itself against the window of the meeting room, its wings raised viciously, beak open, smashing itself again and again against the solar glass.

We try to ignore it, but it doesn't stop. It hisses like a reptile.

'Switch the window to privacy,' I say. The bird is defending itself from its reflection.

'He's trying to destroy the image of himself.'

They look at me strangely when I say this. The select covey of press. Here for facts on the Ice Dock. Given there's a protest march this afternoon against it.

'Why do you assume it's a he?' asks a skinny, nervous-looking guy. Colin, says his lanyard.

'It's a chaffinch,' I say. 'The females are more dull.'

I've found it a useful thing to do. Say something or behave a way that offsides people. Then, when you tell them something sensible it has the added power of surprise.

I look through the glass partition to the worker pool and can't help thinking of slow dinosaurs. A cow-eyed herd, gathered placidly and chewing amongst low tree ferns with vegetarian stupidity.

Every now and then someone reaches for a mug. Like they're picking fruit, foraging amongst felty partitions in the sulphured air, their backs hunched over computers, shirts the grey, pale green and soft pink colours of the skins of wild pigs. All with little socks on.

You can tell a lot about a person from their socks. And their mugs for that matter.

I steer myself away from guessing what underwear everyone is wearing and look up dinosaurs on my selphone. I try to figure out what sort of dinosaurs exactly I'm reminded of. Parasaurs, I find.

Parasaurs (they think) produced low-frequency resonances, rudimentary linguistics rivalling some monkeys. Herding bipeds accumulating in a rigid social hierarchy, with a mid-way intelligence.

Mm.

I have a vague memory of reading somewhere that ninety-nine per cent of species that have ever lived have gone extinct. Or perhaps I heard it on the nature discs. I bought them, a job lot, and the mechanical disc player, from the throwback store. Even the little whirr of the machine is calming. Whhhiiiirrrrrr. Click. Zeeeeeeee.

Last night I watched Emperor Penguins.

They talk in-tow melt rates given the increased salinity and warmer ocean currents and how much of the berg we're likely to lose but how, even so, the maths support bringing it here and that we were right to not dock-build further north and try to move the water overland.

'Look at the trouble they already have with the Water Train,' Alan adds, 'and the increasing attacks.' He seems to aim that at the Westminster spokesperson, and she tenses in her seat, braced to answer questions.

But Alan nods to Susan and she starts the digigram. The visual looks beautiful. Draws all eyes, as Alan starts the fairy tale. How . . .

. . . The floating ice will come up from the coast (he explains) and be linked to the winch . . .

Tap tap. Tap tap.

Still the chaffinch beats the glass.

. . . Then will move on heated rollers that follow the old bed of the river.

Initially, the rollers will warm the bottom of the berg to create a melt zone. The ice above will push down on that zone, creating friction, causing further heat which will, in turn, itself melt the base of the ice, giving it more fluidity to move. The meltwater will be drained to irrigate points along the route, to help grow food.

On the graphic, the process is exaggerated. Gloriously magnified. Over-size drops riddle down the ice, pooling with the water melted by the downward pressure.

My favourite caption appears then on the screen: Stillicide collected to serve crops.

I'd never heard the word before. Stillicide. Water falling, in drops. I challenge myself to get it into a sentence for the pressies.

'Will the Ice Dock only serve the city?' I notice the journalist who asks this wears a blouse the colour of the chaffinch's breast. I've been practising the answer.

'Steven?' Alan invites.

'Yes. Despite the impression, there is actually quite a lot of water to go round. Particularly in the summer.' I make a joke. 'When's the last time you had a barbecue in August?

'There's a lot of rain. And we're an island, so we're surrounded by water we *could* desalinate. But on a large scale, and for so many people, the energy required is prohibitive. When the sun comes out it's hot. But it doesn't come out enough. It's a case, for the smaller communities, of properly managing the water they *do* have.'

'So it's not the fact you can't really own seawater, and so can't make enough money from desalination?' The question comes from Colin. He looks like he eats a lot of kale but not because he likes it.

'No,' I disabuse him. 'It's simply the quantity of people in the city, and what that process would take; and, of course, the quantity of water required for the superfarms that feed us.

'We only drink a relatively small fraction of the supply. Agriculture uses seventy per cent. It's likely part of that draw, over and above the in-transit stillicide (yay!), will be serviced by the Water Train.'

'The term "they" was used earlier, but the corporation own the train as well. Right?' Colin, again.

'We manage the *technical* operation of the train. It's *owned* by the city,' Alan clarifies.

'Which is why the Metropolitan Police patrol the line.'

'Correct. But we're here to talk about the Ice Dock. Not the Water Train.'

'Of course,' Alan picks up, 'the project does mean sacrifices' (why use that word?). 'Not just the Dock itself. The tipping basin the tugs will tow it to, and the conveyor-way to bring the berg into the Dock. All this means moving people. But we're trying to water millions here – and the other benefits that come with this. Some of us' (and why use 'us'?), 'will have to "take one for the team".'

I see the pressies wince at this, but how else can you put it?

Even from primary school science they should know. The weight displaced by a floating object equals the weight of that floating object.

What does an average family weigh?

'Perhaps we should bring Ms Williams in here,' I suggest, and Alan invites the Spokesperson for Westminster to speak.

'Well, yes,' Ms Williams says. 'Government *is* supporting smaller cities, as well as here.' I thought we'd moved on from that question, but. 'Plans for extra reservoirs are already significantly progressed.'

'And people displaced, again.' Colin gives Ms Williams no time to answer. 'As in the 1950s and 60s. Whole communities.'

'You're talking about the bombings then, of dams in Wales that watered Northern and Midland cities.'

'I'm surprised you know. Causing political tension. Militant factions. Just as with the Water Train.'

I have the weird conviction Ms Williams is going to swallow Colin, flick out her tongue like a chameleon, and gulp him down in one.

'There are always people who will look to destabilise society,' she says. (She should have said derail.) 'To create division.'

'When they're pushed to,' Colin says, as if he's proud of them.

'Often because it serves them.' Ms Williams seems unflapped. 'Unfortunately, people will need to be displaced again. But in the case of hillside communities we are rebuilding new settlements. For them to relocate to. Most of them within short distances of their existing homes.'

'Shanty towns! Out of rusty metal boxes.' Colin must be hard to live with.

'The re-use of containers from the decommissioned shipping yards provides a cost-effective and flexible solution with low eco-impact.'

'But you're still displacing families that have lived in a place for generations. Just as with the Ice Dock.'

'Yes. But this is unavoidable. We live in a society. It isn't always possible to take into account every individual. Policy always aims to arrive at a solution which helps the greatest number.'

Here it comes, from Colin . . .

'By definition, then, the cities.'

. . . Setting me up perfectly.

'But this is a key aspect,' I interject, 'of this Ice Dock project. It will serve the city from *within* the city. This won't mean a community of farmers having their way of life destroyed so a distant town can have water. The people affected are from within the community that will benefit. It's time for the city to take responsibility for itself.'

My silver bullet fired I look at the display cases around the room. A beautiful desiccated shoe, the archaeological finds uncovered during the build; the mural of the Dock site through the ages: the tower blocks flattened; Victorian causeways, a medieval bustle; a Saxon settlement upon the fen. The stadium suddenly disappeared, as if it's lifted into space. They all look somehow interchangeable, these times, and humanised. Then there is the big white hole.

Ms Williams speaks passionately, is animated. She looks like a puppet, except she has no strings. Just the muscle memory that's got her where she is.

We see another glorious digigram. A canopy of prisms focus sunlight on the ice. And Susan brings in glasses of cool ice water.

'We want it to be cheap, and available to all,' says Alan. 'And municipal subsidies will help. The Mayor and most people in the city are fully behind the Dock.'

We break up the formal session.

The digigram loops its gorgeous graphics, plays a quiet music, symphonic in its way like the soundtrack of the nature discs.

Another screen gives us a live feed of work in progress at the Dock site. Men busy at the concrete face of the bay, dust rising about them like a smoke. They look more to be attacking the structure than progressing it. Smugglers and bandits, garbed in totem clothes.

'Your background is in oil,' I hear Colin pointedly ask Alan. 'Then you moved into renewables.'

'That was some time ago,' says Alan. Most backgrounds are, I think.

Alan suggests, 'Let's go up to the roof.'

We look over the city, pleasantly drinking our ice waters. The light bends on the solar glass.

Flowers tumble in the gutters.

I can see, from here, some of the homes that will be bulldozed. Beyond them, the great arena of the Dock.

The colourful patches of the shacks in the emptied canals.

The police baffles positioned on the rooftops that overlook the route of the march. The blue caps of the 'Peepers', as we call the marksmen.

The journalist wearing the chaffinch blouse finds herself beside me. I'm staying away from Colin.

'We give a lot,' I take the opportunity to tell her, as she takes in the city from this height. 'That's hard to see sometimes. From ground level.'

I nod out at the rooftop gardens. One nearby blatant with multi-coloured flowers. 'It's great how buildings' residents have come together to make this happen.'

'A lot's got from alittlement.' The journalist beams as she provides the jingle. Sips.

Just below, a rooftop lush with summer vegetable beds.

Below this, in the square outside the building, a crowd no bigger than my palm from here, protestors now have gathered. To picket the office before they head on to the Dock. It's clever of Alan to bring us up here. The march looks dull and diminished. Below the gardens, and the space. The placards too small from this distance to read.

Colin the Skinny has buttonholed poor Ms Williams.

'We're doing something historic here.'

'While making a lot of money.'

'By doing something that will benefit this city for a very long time.'

Clearly he has no sense of wonder.

'And Government won't be making any money. Everyone has access to water, rationed as it may be. But there's only going to be more of us. The icebergs are a ready form of fresh water, and have been very effective in supplying smaller cities on a more modest scale. The current supply is not enough.'

As if in defence of itself, then, far away, and muffled, we hear the Water Train. Its deep boom as it enters the outskirts of the city.

'It's easy to paint us as the bad guys,' I say quietly. Like I'm not trying to make a great big point. To make it clear I am talking more personally to the chaffinch journalist beside me.

'There's a lot of grumbling,' I say. 'But look.'

The rooftops, bright with colour.

'People get on with it. People have always got on with it. Dystopia is as ridiculous a concept as Utopia. Ultimately, we're animals,' I say, thinking of the nature discs. 'And animals find ways.'

The light snaps along the drained riverbed. A bolt of silver ribbon.

I am always astonished from this height, to see how fast new buildings come up. To either side, of course, of the great space of the Dock.

I breathe in. Feel something of the settlement the nature programmes bring. Watch the faint shift of the vapournets on the aircon units.

A slight flutter, like the barest movement inside a chrysalis, as it nears its time to hatch.

The march is underway. Penguins on the move. The chants the walkers call out reach us incoherent and delayed, so the mouths of the walkers, opening and closing, look more to gasp than shout.

'Once you change the idea of what constitutes the ground, we have so much space. You just can't see it from below.'

The journalist beside me traces the drops of condensation beaded on her glass.

'I've never heard that word, stillicide, before,' she says.

'No,' I say. 'Nor had I.'

DRAGONFLY

The professor left the failed hive until last.

The bees were dead around it, curled like dropped alder catkins.

He put the samples into the case. At least the majority of the colonies were healthy. Drawing the honey from them he was reassured by the tight pats on his suit as the returners knocked busily into him.

The fiddly work of fitting tracking wires to the bees was paying off. They could analyse the pollen in the honey in each hive and work out what was growing where. The results had been surprising. All very well, the doom and gloom. But the array of flowering species was astonishing. The city might be grey at ground level, but its rooftops were spectacular with bursts of life and colour. Mostly, the bees weren't even travelling very far.

The failed hive, though, was quiet. The professor took off his hood.

He fingered the dead bees.

The Urbee project was a great success, but there were these troubling random failures.

He knocked the water condensers fitted round the air duct units to check they were working. Watched the bright water work its way along into the vegetable beds.

The courgette plants were celebrant with shameless yellow flowers. He smiled to see the minute pollen beetles in amongst them.

Below, on the streets, he could see the growing crowd gathering to march against the increased scale of the Ice Dock.

Most of his students had absented themselves today. Some, with excuses he wished he could frame. Others had simply been honest. They wanted to walk in protest. And why not, he privately thought.

Granted, they had picked a site that meant the impact on homes was limited. But the Mayor had recently announced they'd also need to clear the flanks of the approach channel. More families would be relocated. It's how they worked. Once a thing was underway, it was very hard to stop. It was a bullying in some ways.

The professor noted the gun baffle on the building roof across the river, sited to overlook the bridge. On its transparent hood, the varnish of its baffle number caught the sun. Baffle three. The dark blue cap of the rifleman as he moved about the roof looked something like a lycaenid butterfly, the professor thought. Purple Hairstreak. In this light.

The professor wasn't sure what one police marksman would be able to do if something did happen while the protest was in sway. Better to have him there than not though, he supposed.

He knew the science of why animals formed groups. But it seemed madness, to him. A crowd was a condensed target, should anybody want to cause them harm.

Better to be better at being a one.

There was a hiss from his comms button.

'Hello.' He pressed the patch.

'There's a parcel for you here, professor.'

With the large bulb of her cycle helmet and the bright material of her clothes, the courier looked like a bee herself. Or, perhaps more a wasp. The way she tapered at the waist.

The professor eyed the parcel, set there on the desk, as he clambered from his bee-keeping suit.

'I hear you on the radio,' said the courier.

Despite himself, the professor couldn't help a little smile. He was unsure about being wheeled out. About being the face of the city's environmental push. Afraid it would mean he had to compromise his opinion. But it had worked well. The rooftops. The diversity. The insect hatcheries in the park.

'I've got a gutter garden on my building,' the courier said, excitedly. 'We group-funded.'

'That's good to know.'

'And we're going to get an alittlement on the roof!'

The professor looked at the package on the desk. An itch in his fingers.

'They'll make a difference.'

'A lot's got from alittlement,' the courier smiled, reeling off the jingle. People called it to him on the street! 'I love your accent,' she said.

That offsided him somewhat.

'Where are you from?' the wasp girl asked.

'North East,' said the professor. 'Near Redcar.'

The package, small as it was, gave the impression it was waiting for him to succumb to its attention with the patient way some cats have.

'There's an ice dock up there, isn't there?'

'One of the small ones,' the professor answered.

```
Incidental report. Student 512. Posting area non-
applicable. Independent study. Dock development
area, grid ref TQ 381837. Solo. Verification
location-tagged visual evidence, embedded.
```

Ellie's voice. Always such a bounce to it.

```
Attendant material, specimen. One. Cast skin,
larval exoskeleton . . .
```

Exuvia, he can't help correcting her. It's an *exuvia* . . .

The extraordinary husk, barely an inch long and caught as if alive in the tube,

```
.  .  . Odonata. Species unconfirmed. Dated as
report.
```

The professor back-swipes.

```
Species unconfirmed. Dated as report.
```

Ellie sent the specimen from a development area near the Dock site. Part of the ground that will become the tow-track along which the iceberg will travel, up from the re-flooded river. The area cleared some two years now. A 'guerrilla' expedition, Ellie jokes, under her own steam.

. . . There's mallow. White dead-nettle. Clematis
(*vitalba*) establishing. 'Old Man's Beard'. I love
that name. Wild clary. Hoverflies, good sign! Can't
see it, but there's a dove somewhere.

Ellie holds the recorder up to catch the coo, but it's faint,
barely perceptible.

Cultivated roses. Hey! A comma. That's beautiful.
On a white buddleia. Some of your bees are here.
I can spot their little wires.

The professor back-swipes again, to where she says, 'a
comma'.

Taps his finger further down the line of the recording.

. . . Ice Dock's huge. Sort of in the distance
but sort of not. It looks like pictures of the
Colosseum!

Taps again.

. . . pile of dust and earth with bits of broken
brick in it. But. So many grasses. Sainfoin. Oh!
Campanula. 'Bellflowers'. They're so pretty, look.
You can eat these, you know. Of course you know.

There are small rustles as she bends to pick a leaf.

Eeek . . . Stealing from a witch's garden . . .
Mmm . . . I can see why Rapunzel's mum went mad
for it . . . Turnipy.

The professor pauses the report, picks up the tube.

The package on the desk, split open down its middle just like
the specimen. This thing of wonder he holds in his hand
emerged from it; and he is startled. As if he has actually
watched it climb from the wrapping and come to him.

Dehiscent, he thinks. Can I use that word for this?

No, that's only plants. The splitting along a built-in line of
weakness in a structure.

An unscientific nervousness starts in the professor's
middle as he looks at the exuvia.

Even with his naked eye he can see. A dragonfly larva in
the last instar. The abdominal barb, he's sure, on the ninth
segment. But the segments are tricky to count with the
eye. And just one skin.

If it's what he thinks it is, they emerge to hatch *en masse*. So.

There must have been more . . .

He forwards to the time stamp Ellie's given in her handwritten note. Odd to find the fact she's scribbled to him with an old-fashioned pen more personal somehow than listening to her voice.

```
. . . old pipe maybe? Don't know. It's got kind
of bust concretey edges. Definitely some sort of
pipe.
```

Swimming beetles. Insects on the water. Pond skaters, Gerridae. And whirligigs. That's another name I love. 'Whirligigs.' Quite a few. Don't like my shadow, shy little things. Imagine breathing through your bum! Different types of waterweed. Gnats!

Gnats. What sort of gnats? *Sylvicola*? *Macrocera*?

```
There's a pile of chunks stacked up. Look more
soily than concretey, really. Does that make
sense?
```

It's clay. It's a clay sewer pipe.

```
It is sort of dug down to. As if the ground has
collapsed a bit.
```

The professor feels a kind of flutter in his centre. An expectation, that Ellie's next few details will confirm the leap of imagination he's not been able to prevent. That this 'pipe' is one of the many waterways they culverted, or co-opted as sewers, and built the growing city over, in the 1800s.

There's big old flag iris to one side. The stalks all dried out. It's in the sun. Nearly midday now.

Ellie, Ellie, tell me. Was the water *running*?

Oh! Hang on.

Even barely?

That's. Wow! Yes! It's a skin . . .

Exuvia . . .

It has the look of a shrunk dragon. A frail ferocity to its proportions. The heavy intent of its head. Its front two pairs of legs extended forward, as if it reaches out to claim something.

He places the cast skin on the plate of the field microscope. Focuses.

The mud of the pool bottom has dried upon the skeleton, an arid silt. He cannot help but think of ash. A rebirth. The body split, the soul escaped on wings.

There is something about the mud that gives the look of interruption. He recognises he is thinking of Pompeii. Perhaps because of Ellie's mention of the Colosseum. Of people stopped mid-process.

Again, the scientist, he thinks of souls. Of a great heat vaporising the essence from a body.

The dorsal barbs, down to the penultimate section of the abdomen. The fact of the dried silt. He has pushed back the prospect. An intuition of its species he felt instantly.

But as he sees the skin, magnified, it speaks to him as an artefact. Seems utterly sure of itself. It *is*.

The barb on the ninth segment.

Libellula fulva. 'Scarce Chaser'. Dragonfly. Unmistakable.

He looks to the date on the record he's called up. The last recorded sighting. UK-wide. More than twenty years ago . . . On the drains of the Ouse Washes.

It's on the Red List of protected species. As he thought it might be.

He gazes through the binocular field microscope.

It's not the same, to him, to use the digital scopes. He was drawn to *things*. *Things* had given him wonder, and he was a scientist because of that, not for the need to understand. He tried to instil that in his students.

For him, the search was not answers, the search was for surprise.

Does Ellie know? Does she know the significance of this?

A dragonfly. A predator at the top point of a triangle. On the Red List. One of the few things the countries of the world agree on.

If a Red List species is present in a place, no action can be carried out that will disturb it until it has been relocated or moved on.

He dials Ellie. Needs to ask. Were there more exuviae?
The water, was it running? Slowly? At all? But gets her
ansaphone.

Ellie here. Can't talk right now. I'm walking
against the Ice Dock project. You should be too.
Leave a message if you want.

Ellie, Ellie, he thinks. Were there more exuviae? Was the
water running . . .?

Turns back to her recording.

Yay! Hopscotch. Kids must come out here to play.

He goes, without any need for conscious navigation, to the
specimen vault, to the section 'Odonata'. Logs on, keys
the species number. 'Odonota' – from the Greek belief
that dragonflies had teeth . . . presses Confirm.

The drawer emits a gentle beep and slides itself open.

A few metres down the vault, the integral inspection light
casts a knee-high glow, and he feels a hum as he crouches
to see the specimen, as if he finds it in the field.

There, vibrant under the light, Scarce Chaser. *Libellula fulva*. Male.

The powder-blue pruinescence of its abdomen. A wingspan the length of his thumb. Brown pterostigma. Veins as frail as a leaf skeleton.

He draws the hand lens from his chest pocket. His thumb tracing the comfortable scratch of the long-smoothed inscription on its case.

From above, the dragonfly's eyes are a bottomless blue-grey. Seem gauzed, like the veil of his bee-keeping suit.

Dragonfly, he thinks. Savours their names. 'Devil's Darning Needle'. 'Adderbolt'. 'Ear Cutter'. Their strange helicopter movements, clicking as they take smaller insects in the air.

It's almost impossible for him not to think that this imago clambered from the very skin he holds. The skin he could not leave behind him on his desk. That it crawled somehow from the accumulated silt in which for two years it fed and grew, and that this bright thing in the drawer broke from it.

That must happen. Mustn't it? A dragonfly must land, sometimes, next to the skin of itself it crawled from.

Can they know?

He wants to pick it up and set it on his finger. But does not.

And suddenly and certainly he understands he's going out there. Now. Out to the site where this was found.

That he'll pack his field bag in a rush and go. Take the sampling rods, and nets.

That he will lie down on his belly and plunge his arm into the water.

This species lays its eggs in running water . . . The larvae two years in the silt. Before they clamber up and split.

And if the water is running, it is possible the egg or larva was just carried to the spot. To the break in the pipe. That it's simply an anomaly.

But the Red List is the Red List. And *if* there *are* eggs, or larvae there, work at the site will have to pause.

It wasn't that he was against the Ice Dock. He understood necessity.

But, what this specimen could represent. How it could fire people's engagement.

A silverfish under a mat. A marigold established in the crack of a kerb. The belligerent will of a thing to exist.

Give Nature space, and she will take it.

What a story it would make.

What half a million people on the march will not achieve, a tiny insect might.

A dragonfly could stop an iceberg.

For a while at least.

ROOFTOP

When the service door opened, a falcon burst away from the gun baffle. A brief blur that seemed to stay in the air long after it was gone. Leave the space it occupied more present. The way the doctor's words had hung there in the air.

'Keen eyes,' said the constable who had brought Branner up in the access lift.

Branner nodded; then he checked his rifle and stepped onto the roof.

He knew he'd see her ward from here. Did not look towards the hospital.

He'd asked to be posted out of the city. To spend a few days at the Water Train line. To find some space, to try to settle with things.

'We'll need you for the protest, though. You can go out to the line for the next rota. If the Super clears it.'

A few more days, thought Branner. Then I'll be out there. There'll be some time to set things straight in my head.

'You go,' said his wife. She understood.

The transparent shell of the baffle deflected the cool wind. Deepened Branner's feeling he was in a bubble.

The dream, recurring night after night, now seemed an intuition. After the doctor's news.

With his feet off the roof Branner seemed to float, rode a momentary swoon of vertigo.

Let the process take over, he coached himself. Use the process.

He set the rifle in the rest. Checked the pneumatics. Steered the baffle left, right, nodded and tipped it with the foot pedals.

Let the spin of unease pass.

He clipped the umbilica from the rifle to his chestconnect, felt, for a very strange moment, he attached a line to his heart. Then he engaged the comms and spoke into the headset. 'In place.'

There was endless movement below, between the solid, impassive buildings.

On the distant flat roofs Fillic sheets caught the afternoon light.

Branner took things in. The resting meter of the city.

Ahead of him the bridges, on which the protest would converge to cross the empty river channel over to the Ice Dock.

Behind him the hospital.

Left of the bridge the Ice Dock itself. Dust from the construction work within lifting from it like faint smoke.

Between the dry riverbed and the Dock was derelict ground. Bulldozered leftovers of cleared buildings piled around the site.

Branner scoped the area. A huge space but dwarfed by the Dock. The land of the old park behind.

Despite the high fences, there were signs of people. Spent fires. A hopscotch court. Graffiti.

Untidy patches of silver-grey scrub.

The broken opening in the waste ground caught him unawares. A memory that flipped his stomach. The dark opening like a section of blown-out pipe.

It brought a sudden bile of adrenalin into Branner's mouth. His pulse thickened and he felt the walls of detachment shudder.

What was it?

He increased the magnification of his scope. It looked as if something heavy had fallen through the floor.

From the sporadic growth around it, Branner sensed the hole held water.

He felt the adrenalin turn soupy inside him.

Tried to call up a sharpness, to cut through the film that, since this morning, the doctor's words had created between him and the rest of the world.

He wanted a jolt. Some flash to bring him back to earth. Hoped quietly for a crisis. Something that would require his whole mind.

A soft pulse in the chestconnect directed Branner to check the sectors he hadn't yet. He swung the baffle. Had to. And there some quarter-of-a-mile away was the hospital. Like a cliff.

Through the scope he saw the square-looking white beds. The uniforms of the senior nurses the same blue as his police marksman cap. Not like the pale blue she'd worn the first time they met. Sewing up the wound in his jaw.

Branner wanted to stare the hospital down. Had the insane thought he could shoot the building dead and put an end to things. That if he killed the building, all the illness in it would be done.

There was the falcon again, on the building's roof. A bolt-black silhouette the size of a bullet casing, against the pale squat structures of the windtwist generators.

He eyed it in the scope. Brought it bold and tangible. Alive with colour, detailed. Close. Then, as if aware of him, it dipped off the ledge, the sudden engine of its shoulders driving it into the sky and out amongst the buildings.

Branner turned away from the hospital. A scruffy dog trotted across the waste ground, stopped briefly and periodically to sniff, to mark. Went instinctively to the broken shallow and lowered its head to drink. Water.

The dog looked feral. It had the thick head and shoulders of an aggressive dog, but an energetic gait.

The dog brought scale to the ground. The fallaway section looked some three to four metres in length and half that wide.

Branner watched the dog, the skin around the scar on his jaw tacking slightly against the rifle stock.

It had a calm certainty. Dipped its head to drink again.

A little way from the pool sparrows folded in the dust.

The thin needling cry of a swift scratched the air.

They had hoped for rain, to diminish somewhat any casual enthusiasm for the protest. But the sun had got stronger through the afternoon, and the heat began to come up off the roof and catch under the hood.

Branner took some of his water ration.

'Baffle nine,' came Control.

'Check,' said Branner.

There was the soft white noise of electric traffic, filtered through the city. The sun flashed on the perimeter fence below.

Then Branner saw a small boy clamber through the failure in the panel and run, in a headlong way, towards the dog.

The boy too looked feral. He would be seven or eight, guessed Branner.

Before the boy could get to the dog, the dog bounded away. Then stopped. Turned.

Barks reached Branner out of synch with the snaps of the dog's jaw.

The dog was playing, but the boy seemed distraught. Gave loose, frustrated flaps of his arms, as if he tried uselessly to leave the ground.

The dog was delighted. Rolled in the dust. Stretched in the sun. Approached.

But every time the young boy took a step, the dog ran away.

In the end, the boy sat down in the dirt.

Branner saw the fence ripple again. The second boy had snagged his clothing. His face, in the globe of Branner's scope, was angry and flushed. No more than a few years older than the first boy. He looked asthmatic, Branner thought.

There was some chatter on the comms, but Branner kept his focus on this second boy. The boy had torn his football shirt getting through the fence and shouted across the waste ground. He clenched and unclenched his fists as he walked.

It was clear the boys were brothers.

When the younger brother got up from the dirt, the older brother held him by the arm, and the dog barked once, percussively, as if something had been dropped.

Then the smaller boy began to bawl words into the other's face. It seemed to pummel the older boy.

It was strange to see. Not hearing anything, at the distance Branner was from them.

Something, then, came across the children.

The dog became compressed and stiff, stared tensely past the boys. Growled, inaudibly to Branner. The minutest shake. Then it uncoiled and hammered off towards the empty river.

Branner looked to see what had caused the dog to spook. The younger boy already ran and shouted after it. The older pleading, hardly able to lift his feet.

Branner leant to the scope and went about a rhythmic grid check, sure he'd see another dog. Or people. Did not. Checked the waste ground patch by patch.

When he looked up, having done so, both the boys were gone.

People threaded onto the bridge. Surchins larked in the concrete channel below.

Branner looked to recognise the two brothers amongst them but did not. He looked for the dog.

The light gleamed off the mica held in the dry sandy mud.

The soft crunching chant of the protest came to him now, guided between the buildings, filling the streets ahead of the marchers.

It brought Branner the sense of something rolling, clanking towards him. He saw the bridge like a funnel.

When he looked back at the waste ground, as if he sensed him first, Branner saw the man.

He lay on his belly, an arm outstretched in the water. Branner's stomach twisted again, upturned.

Light bounced from the weapon the injured man had dropped. It seemed he tried to drag himself.

Branner feared, for a horrible moment, that he'd had some sort of absence, during which he'd shot the man. The way the man lay prone.

He felt a sort of clatter in his brain. The off-synch patter of the protest growing more defined; the travel of the Overland that passed along the bridge.

From the deep hollow inside himself, Branner heard the doctor's words begin again to knock and rattle. An expectation; some object tumbling closer.

A wash of adrenalin came with a taste like the metal smell of sundered iron. And his body braced.

He waited for this morning's news to reach him.

The horrible moment, waiting for the doctor's words to detonate.

'Baffle nine.' Comms call cutting through the chemical flood.

'Check,' said Branner.

But he was back, now, there. His first posting. Barely old enough to leave the base. Pulling bodies from the pooling water of the sabotaged pipeline.

How they'd stood there, helpless, listening, the next bomb pinging and clanging towards them down the pipe.

It was that day. That day at the pipe you met.

He brought his eyes down onto the protest. Went for the safety of the scope. But.

'Sir.'

'What is it?'

'I'm not fully with this, sir.'

'Branner?'

'I'm not focused, sir.'

'We can't bring you down now. Are you fit for a shot?'

'I don't think so, sir.'

'You've got the bridge, John. There's a reason it's you up there.'

'She's not going to come through.'

For a moment all he could acknowledge was the sky, the wide sky.

'Switch off your gun, Branner.'

'It's okay. I've said it now.'

'Switch your gun off, John.'

'No, sir. I'm good. I just needed to say it. There was a falcon on the roof, sir.'

'Branner.'

'I'm fine, sir.'

A flock of pigeons bloomed into the space above the building, the falcon toying lazily amongst them. Twisting and tilting. As if called by Branner.

'I'm fine, now, sir. I've said it.'

One of the pigeons seemed to glint with a copper sheen as the flock disappeared.

Branner went for the scope. Like he could miniaturise himself and climb within it, out of view.

A cool air. Wind sharpening.

The metal smell of his rifle.

He saw the man on the waste ground lift himself and lean back, hold something to the light. Saw it was not a weapon beside the man but a rod of some type. Some scientific thing.

It will be legit, Branner thought. Some survey. Something to do with the Dock.

There was a hiatus. Branner stayed in the scope, watched the man unpack vials, tubes. Reach for the strange rod.

Thought of the calm procedural tone the doctor used this morning, to break the news. His wife would die.

He saw then the younger boy, down on the empty riverbed. Throwing stones at the Overland as it passed above him. The scruffy thick-set mongrel dizzy round the boy's feet.

Focus, John.

The hospital behind him.

The scene below an object now. A coin through a jeweller's loupe.

Watch the bridge, he coached himself. Focus on the bridge.

The protest now was filtering. The crowd seeming to pour.

Something microscopic in the fact the smallest tap could send a hundred-and-seventy-grain bullet three-quarters of a mile.

Move your finger just a millimetre and you could end a life; but you cannot save one. Her. Not with the strength of your whole body.

Branner felt himself sliding again, away from the wider world. Into the big hole in his ground, the time ahead without her.

The pull of the chasm.

You need to focus now.

She is fading, you can feel it.

And there is nothing you can do.

Come on, he thought, come on. Happen, something, so I do not have to think of her.

Lake

After the deafening noise and the cool dark of the pumphouse it took Cora a moment to adjust to the relative quiet and the bright sun.

It seemed impossible that the noise of the gravity loaders deep in the rock could barely be heard from outside. But they gave now only a low thrum.

Cora blinked in the light. Butterflies batted their wings as they sunned themselves on the wall of the pumphouse entrance.

There was the self-contained hum of the hoses as the train took on water.

Above the pumphouse, on the slope of the mountain, the gorse was egg-yolk thick. Pale sheep stood out against the grass.

Beyond the scrub and the scattered rock, the wall of the dam looked medieval. Geometric. Impassive.

It looked somehow far older than the mountain.

On the brow of the slope, like shepherds, were the wolf-grey figures of two guards.

The cloth tacked slightly to the ice as Cora adjusted her grip on the block she had brought from the pumphouse cavern.

They had collected the ice from the reservoir in January, those that were here over Christmas, stood to their waists in frozen shore water, pickaxing away.

They stacked the ice in a fissure in the cavern, on a metal grid so its meltwater could drain. As best they could, diverted the stillicide that slid down the face of the rock.

Now, in late summer, they still had ice.

Remembering was odd in this heat. That January day the first time she noticed Leo properly.

The languid way he wielded the pick. A sort of liquidity to it.

She did not think she was a body person. But. His had surprised her.

All the science here. All the tech. The astonishing engineering of burrowing through ancient rock to connect pipes to the floor of a full reservoir. And to keep their beers cool, it came down to a pickaxe. Not that, in that freezing January, any of them could imagine it would ever be warm again.

The sun though, now, was fierce. The only evidence of last night's rain a grateful lushness in the leaves.

It was the first night Cora had spent alone for some time and she lay awake listening to it drum on the eco-foil walls of the pod.

The rain had been brief and heavy.

They needed it. The reservoir was low.

Now, the late-morning heat shimmered off the body of the train.

Cora understood the differentials. The load temperatures inside the vacuum wagon; how condensation formed immediately as the tanks filled; how the friction of the travelling train affected its surface temperature.

She felt she knew the train in some ways, as if it was a living thing.

She could not get used to the guns, though. They were as foreign and recent as the guards.

Cora thought of the cold water deep in the reservoir, loosing into the gravity feeders. Saw it, in her mind, as a liquid dark and slumbering, suddenly energised and burst into a white tumbling rush. Something passive and silent abruptly breaching with unbridled noise.

That was her thing. Latent capacities. The potential of a material to change the form of its energy.

Hence this block of ice. Hence this afternoon's project. Leo did not believe it could be done.

It made more sense to collect the flowers first, but Cora knew that once the train was loaded, the mechs would be in the pumphouse, and she wasn't in the mood for Ryan. Ryan would know Leo was away.

She could do without whatever mean little thing he'd do if they met. Whatever sharp little reminder.

He'd got worse since she and Leo had given up trying to pretend things were just casual, and Leo'd moved in with her.

She was still partly surprised. A year ago, she wanted more than anything to transfer to the Ice Dock project. Perhaps, she wondered now, to get away from Ryan. And then this thing with Leo happened. Quite by surprise. And. The idea of playing with icebergs melted away. She was happy.

She left the block of ice in the cloth on the kitchenette table and put on a summer dress.

Then she put on her walking boots.

She felt like her six-year-old self, going outside in the sun in wellies.

As she stepped out, the air suddenly seemed emptied. The sharp calls of the songbirds quiet. Moments later, the sheep began to wheel on the hill. Moan.

A bumblebee circled with an incongruous drone.

Then the faintest sing came to the wire stays of the accommopods, and the valley filled with the sound of the train starting up.

By the time Cora reached the foot of the hill, the sound was no more than a lessening hush, fading towards the city, hundreds of miles away.

Cora's dress stuck a little to her skin.

Delicate yellow day-flying moths flew amongst the gorse.

There was a heady coconut smell to the flowers. She picked them and dropped them into the bowl. Patient when she pinned her finger. Sometimes felt showered seeds on her skin. Took a while to link the tickle to the spiky, sporadic pops, punctuations in the air, as the flat, mature pea-pods on the bushes burst in the sun.

She gently pinched the part-closed petals together and pulled; took soft buds, the faint hairs between her fingers, like stroking a small animal's ear.

Below her, in the bowl of the valley, the foil of the accommopods gleamed like mica. The tech buildings looked no bigger than the squat, low boxes of the bumblebee hives she'd passed on her way up the hill.

Every now and then there was a quiet bump of rabbits.

She was at the same time a long way away and very here. Deeply thoughtful, but content.

Her mind went easily from one thing to another. Rested sometimes. Waited. Flitted.

She thought of Leo.

She thought of lunch.

She thought of raw grated carrot fresh from the nearby farm. The difference the new-farm being here had made. As had the chickens the crew had decided to take on, managing the care by rota and sharing out the eggs. The veg patch they had not quite got to grips with yet.

Thought of how dry the grass was and how she should have put on sun lotion.

And then they were suddenly there.

She jumped. Hard and jolting. A horrible zip through her system.

The two guards stood above her, stepped from the thorn.

Cora felt sick.

She had jumped hard enough to spill gorse around her feet.

She followed the gaze of one of the guards, who looked at the flowers on the ground.

When she looked back, he held her eye.

'Farm?' he said.

'No. I'm with the train. I'm off shift,' she felt the need to say.

She wished she had her pass. As if it could protect her. As if it could ward them off.

'What are you doing up here?' asked the guard.

'I'm making ice cream,' said Cora. It made no sense.

The guard stared at the bowl of flowers in her hand. The flowers dropped around her feet.

Her walking boots. Her legs.

'What do you do with the train?'

'Thermo.'

The thinner guard reviewed her with strange unbatting eyes. 'I've seen you. I've noticed you,' he said. And it felt as if his eyes rolled into the bowl of her mouth.

Cora felt an animal certainty that there were more men than there really were.

Her dress clung to her sweat. She felt it outline her. Present her.

'You should not be up here,' said the first guard.

The locus of her fear changed. To a fear they were going to mete out punishment.

'There are people. Up here,' the guard continued. 'They have intent. It's why we're here. You can't be up here.'

Cora felt the eyes of the thinner guard in the soft shallow of her neck.

'Have you not read the directives?'

'Best go back,' said the first guard.

Cora could not stop the shake. It set the gorse buds rattling in the bowl.

'We'll pretend this didn't happen.'

Her dress stuck to the sweat of her skin.

'Read the directives.'

The yolks were the colour of a bumblebee's band. The mix paling and thickening as she beat them with sugar.

The claim there were people up there, out there, on the hill, waiting to attack. Directives. Tear-proof clothes, equipment vests and heavy boots. And guns.

Her adrenalin had morphed into a frustrated anger.

They were not needed here. Everything here had been quiet. Chicken runs. The gleam of eco-foil accommopods. A nearby new-farm and ice stashed in a hill. It was good here.

Now them. The guards had simply been surreal to her.

And now.

As she infused the syrup, the faint smell of gorse got into the kitchenette. As if she was still up there in the thorn.

When she unwrapped the block of ice to break it up, the cloth again clung briefly.

Her dress bunched, strewn now, in the basket for the drywash.

Don't. Don't let it spoil it. She talked to herself. They were just doing their job. They just surprised you.

But it was done.

When she went out later, the block of ice sat melting slowly into the border at the edge of the path. The bowl of glaceous egg whites in the fridge reminded her it was her night to close up the chickens.

She'd got angrier. The way, when she'd turned to look from the foot of the hill, she saw them, sat as if for a picnic, watching her through their rifle sights.

Nothing happened, she kept telling herself that.

You were being silly.

But it had spoiled it. She was sure her anger would taint the eggs and sugar.

Had dumped the mixture in the waste.

Thrown the block of ice into the flowers, where it still sat resisting the sun. Melting stubbornly.

Leo'll still be a while, she told herself. There's still time. He'll be a while before he's home.

He was worried about his parents. They lived right by the coast, and the land was falling away. They would not move.

There's still enough ice.

Use his solar drill to break it up, with one of the chisel fittings. Or his fossil hammer. Like a mini pickaxe.

She'd expected clothes, and big shoes, and perhaps a favourite mug to find their way into her place; but chiefly he'd filled the place with tools. And unexpected curious things. The tiny red and white lighthouse he had treasured since a child. An architect's scale model of a section of the water pipeline his father had worked on years ago. Bags of salt his parents sent, that they scraped from their desalinator. That she had intended to scatter on the ice. To speed the melt and heat transfer.

She pictured how beads of condensation would form around the outside of the aluminium bowl, as it did against the body of the train.

He will be tired. And you could give him hand-made ice cream. From ice he pickaxed from a reservoir.

There's still time, she said to herself. Come on. Be brighter. They just surprised you. Close the chickens first.

The hens were bunched on perches. After the dry day, there was a faint ammonia smell.

With the sun dropped, it was colder than Cora had expected. There were goosebumps on her skin.

The sheep out on the hill looked like dull patches of dropped paper. A minerally white like the inside of the eggshells.

Cora thought of the reservoir. The deep prehistoric patience of the water hung there in the hill above.

Felt a sudden increased chill. The landscape darkening away into the twilight. The dam like some strange impassive eyelid in the mountain.

Then she heard the click. Snap.

The hens bridled. Unfurled, and clucked quietly, quick gulps they swallowed in their neck.

There, with impossible solidity, was a figure. A face, dark with mask, that bore into Cora, and she felt her centre drop out, as the door of the run banged, and she was caged, with the crack of the latch, rocking.

And someone was there. Loomed. Gloved fingers curled around the wire, the black absence of a face; began to shake the run. And talk. And tell her.

We'll take the train. We'll take the train. We're going to take the train.

Then he was gone, into the night.

Sound

The calf gave a confused hiss, and lowing, then dipped slightly as if it would bury into the water.

When the second harpoon hit, thumping its flank a second later, it seemed to groan somewhere deep within itself. A contained sound of suffering such that it was impossible not to believe the thing understood. That it was young and had a sense of the freedom and scale before it, and that this was now done.

The men in the small boats some twenty metres away braced because they knew the harpoon could put such sudden energy into the calf that it could fly at them, and that men were killed that way. Either from the direct strike or by being upturned. All they had between them and the freezing water was the five metres of Hypalon-coated polyester.

There were three men in each boat.

After the initial cowering, barely noticeable in normal time, the men recovered. All of this happened in a matter of moments. They drove the boats away, the twisted-steel harpoon lines, awkward and heavy, playing out behind.

The water was so flat it felt thick, and they – the only disturbance in it – seemed more to plough than to float through its surface. They went slowly.

The sound of the motors snapped in the air as if some communication took place between the boats.

They used modified old D-class RIBs, with big fifty-horsepower outboards. The outboards were disproportionate on the back of the inflatables but balanced by the heavy harpoon gun in the prow, and to an extent the weight of the wire lines.

At the hundred-metre knot the Lead Man called a stop.

There was still a chance the calf could blast at them and they had to suppress their instinct to put distance down quickly. But the most dangerous thing was done.

Each of the crew tried to divine what state the calf was in, watching it as if they could ascertain intention.

The boats wallowed.

The tock of their idling motors beat out into the open space. Somehow, the noise seemed to confirm the potential for profound quiet here. This sat too in the men, beneath the thoughts they were having, their estimations of remuneration. The fact one of them was madly hungry.

'Ready the anchor,' the Lead Man said.

'Four hundred,' the harpooner said, and the Lead Man nodded. He looked to the other boat. A hand went up in answer.

The red coats they wore were extremely bright with the sun so clear.

The Lead Man held his thumb and finger in the air before him in a backward C, as if he could squeeze the calf and lift it from the water.

He calculated its size, pushed his thumb into his nose, a thing he did, and nodded again. Should it spin on them, they were clear.

'Just to the left. Hit it there.'

121

The thermal anchor hissed away, turning the air into a stream of steam, hitting the calved ice with a crack that made all the men momentarily sick.

They could not see it, but they pictured the anchor thumping a few lengths into the berg then dropping into its body; a strange conflict of heat, it melting and sinking into the ice, but battled, with the deep cold closing round it, refreezing, setting it inside solidly.

The berg gave a distraught boom, a strangled sound of grief that echoed over the water.

'She's a beauty,' said the harpooner.

'A beauty. All the way blue.'

~

They attached the tow lines to the tugs and the RIBs were winched up in the davits, throwing a shadow on the flat water as they hung like things caught in the talons of a bird.

The main line went to the stronger boat that would take the berg eventually all the way to the dock.

For the first stage of the journey, the two smaller tugs would flank the main tug, adjusting as necessary to keep the iceberg stable as it melted somewhat with manoeuvre and the friction of saltwater.

As they secured the tow lines, the men looked up to the wheelhouse of the main tug; and when they were all aboard the main tug to eat before setting south, they looked at the wheelhouse.

Eventually, the captain came out. He'd checked the sonograph, and made calculations, and by now brokered the ice.

'She's one hundred and ten. That's six hundred and thirty-four barrels. Good leading edge, so there won't be overmuch friction; she shouldn't waist too much. She's a funny shape, but she'll hold.'

'Like your wife,' one of the men muttered, to muffled delight.

'We had two bids. The gallon price was higher south of Dogger. But we'll lose more in the water and she'll likely end up fetching the same. So we're best going short. We also had an offer to park it. How do you feel about that?'

The crew heckled, with mixed accents, unanimously, at the idea. Blunt in their opinions about letting the thing melt to keep prices up.

'Then we'll take her into Redcar. With the melt, means you'll only have to go as far as Sumburgh maybe. This'll take her from there. We're promised a calm sea.'

~

The thick smell of oil and grease came up from the dismantled outboards that lay in pieces about the deck.

The pieces lay like artefacts; the crew's care of them akin to the careful homage of archaeologists.

They scraped away corrosion and the salt, with affection close to love.

Treated the motors as things that were amongst the last of their kind.

'There's no bomb big enough to blow a berg that big,' said the big Icelander.

'They blow themselves easy enough,' to laughter.

'Like someone I know . . .' retort.

'Well. Why would you want to, really?' asked the strange Moroccan.

'To blow up the city!' They were used to the harpooner making statements like this now.

'You wouldn't blow the city up. You'd just shower it in snow,' the Lead Man said.

'The city is a mewling infant.'

'The city, the city.' The Moroccan's clipped-sharp sing-song sound.

'Take, take, take. Imagine how much there'd be to go around. If the cities were just . . . pwff. If they were all just popped, like the bladders on seaweed.'

'He has a point.'

'He has an illness.'

The Icelander said, 'Pass me more bread.'

Behind the boat, the calved berg waited to be towed away, a passive shadow thrown before it on the water.

There was a sense of unrealness to it. Perhaps because it was hard to believe the ice, that looked so fresh and newly formed, was a thousand years old.

~

'Check the specimen drags,' the captain said, and the two men on rota went to it.

'There's never anything,' the Moroccan complained, he and the other hauling the heavy seine, hand over hand. The light plankton net already lifted, draped there by their feet.

But when the net came up there was a fish as thick and long as a man's arm.

A pale subdued gold, the colour of early-morning light on soft flat water. A surprising whisker on its chin.

The fish was inert in the net, placid, and, they assumed, dead. Heavy and arched as if in a hammock.

But as they went to lift it, it flapped. They screamed like girls. A sudden life was in its eyes; some internal energy switched on; and at once it became like a pennant snapping and curling in the wind. Chewing at the air.

When they got it on the deck it stilled again, but for its mouth, small rhythmic gasps, as if it counted down silently the last moments of its life. It thudded once, with a sound on the deck like the thwack of wet rope. Then its counting seemed to slow.

It was the first large fish they'd caught.

'Shall we enter it into the record?' the crewman asked.

'Fetch a knife,' the captain said.

~

The guts slid from the incision as if in surprise; blood that was almost black leaching over the deck. The men now were like children as they watched.

It did not seem possible the guts had been contained within the fish. They came out in handfuls of alien shapes and colours that seemed to bear no relation to the lithe thing lain there split now at their feet.

They did not know, the captain nor the men, to keep the milts, nor liver. The insides hit the water like a jellyfish.

'Do we leave the head on?' someone asked.

The captain said they did.

The head now seemed disproportionate. Like the outboards on the RIBs.

They could cut the fish up and fry it in the small pans they had. But this did not feel right.

One or two of the crew, seeing the fish already diminished, felt privately sad, and the notion of further dismemberment seemed undignified.

They looked at the captain for he was Captain.

Rightly, the fish should be cooked intact.

Then came a moment of small genius.

They wrapped the fish in a foil survival blanket from the boat's First Aid supplies. Then slid it into the barrel of the thermal harpoon gun.

All this was done with a degree of melancholy ceremony, as if they aimed to fire the fish beshrouded out to sea in funeral.

But they set the barrel heat to one hundred and sixty and stood back.

I suppose we give it forty minutes, the captain guessed. 'Give it forty minutes.'

~

When people imagine being out here, they imagine silence, quiet.

But there's the engines. The constant struggle, noise of the engine, pulling.

Never been able to zone it out. Then again, you listen. It's like you see with your ears, not your eyes. The sea ahead, if it's still, doesn't change much to the eye. But you can hear the current thicken, in the engine sound; you can hear a drop in pressure coming, with the sound changing in the air. Even the pull of the wind, the way the sounds are taken.

When the soft tugs are clear we idle a while, exchange banter. Shouting from deck to deck. Watch the counterweights take the tow lines down under the water; the spin of the winches as they wind back in. Their pitch getting higher the less line. Then they change to the lighter solar engines, and head away. The smell of diesel drops from the air. I hear them for far longer than I see them.

When they're out of earshot I cut the motor. I know this should not be done. It's when you can lose a berg, without the movement through the water keeping it stable.

But I do it just to hear the silence. Just a little while.

It's something that if you've never heard you will not understand.

The sound of silence on the Northern water; and the sound of ice. A berg calving away from some great body.

Like something falling from the face of the Earth.

~

He thinks again of heading away, to somewhere without such constant sound.

The long trips have given him time to make all the calculations. How many tins of food he could amass and store in the hold of the boat, and how long they would feed him. The drums of fuel.

Ironically, the problem would be water.

But it could be done.

How far could he get burning the fuel it would take to tow enough ice to keep him; and where would he go? For silence.

He imagines understanding the world with his eyes again. Having to account contours, and colours, and the solidity of a surface.

A picture of himself, in silence, on a flat sea, a raft of birds beside the boat, and the only sound the knock of his spoon against the edge of a tin of food.

But he knows, as he nears the sea defences, sees the panels moulded from the shredded blades of old wind turbines. He would never do that to the men.

131

Not with the chance he's been offered, now, to steer the giant city berg.

It will be historic, he knows. I am the best man for the job. And it will make us rich.

The lights of the dock in the falling light.

But the silence, he thinks. The silence.

POTATO WATER

The sound of vegetables being chopped.

He found the boy in the garden. Curled up like a millipede in the leaves.

The boy was in fever, and sang a song, and talked about his little brother, and a missing dog.

Gone only to collect vegetables; but he brought back a child. There is a fairy tale I remember about that. That my Awa used to tell me.

If I am asked what it is I love most about my husband I say the smell of soil on his hands.

I think if I bit into him he must have the taste of fresh vegetables.

Every day he goes. His garden. That he has dug out at the base of the filtration mound. Rich soil, he says. And moisture. We pretend not to think about why.

Every day he is amazed that no one has stolen the crop. Does not understand how others are not growing things for themselves there too.

It is a filtration mound, I say. And he narrows his brow in bafflement, and rubs his hands, which I think is what pushes the scent of the soil into his skin.

There were butterflies in the rushes today, he tells me.

There are thick white grubs in the earth.

A flame lit, and a pan put on to boil.

~

Drink, I say. Three days now. Nothing but potato water.

The warm steam smells of soil, as if my husband's in the room.

How is he? he asks when he comes back from the garden.

He is thin, the boy. A collection of poles.

~

They followed the dog out of the city. This is what I understand. The dog they had found (and this is my make-believe, but who knows, I may be right) by the bins of a restaurant, when they were stealing the half-used blocks of soap, and part-empty bottles of expensive alcowash, miniature pouches of tooth powder. To sell and to swap with a child's bright way with business.

It was love at first sight. The little brother and the dog. They were both scruffy, and moody, and never behaved. Again, that is my imagination.

But you can read a lot from such a small amount of a person. Rightly or wrongly. Or maybe that is wrong to say. It's not that you read, but you write. You take the tiniest thing you see, and that starts the story of them. The only thing that stops that is to know. For sure. The truths.

I see them clearly. In amongst the shanties and the stalls of the old canal beds. In amongst the shouts and shamming. A defiant little boy with his chest pushed out, trying to be bigger, walking along with the dog at his heels.

And the older brother. Tall and cowed as he is. Not that I have seen him on his feet. A frown I do not think will pass with the fever.

A boy who constantly opens and closes his fists, like he is lifting and letting go over and over again of a responsibility he doesn't have any choice about.

I cannot think about him any other way than as an orphan . . .

Ah! What a time. The lovely stink of the drained canals. Floors from old pallets. Thrown away carpets we took from the emptied houses. Before they knocked them down to build the higher flats.

How we poured, so many of us, into the space. How we so colourfully flowed.

There is no other place he can come from, this boy.

The sound of vegetables being chopped. A radio in the background.

~

I misremembered. It is not that a child is found in the vegetable garden. It is that a child is taken in payment for the theft of rampion . . .

Or, Rapunzel, as they call it.

The child is taken away.

~

It is dark before my husband comes home.

He looks drawn and tired when he does. For once he is not carrying vegetables.

I did not find him, he says.

Did you think that you would?

I can tell that he did. He is that type of man.

Their dog ran off. They went after it, out of the city. He followed his little brother, I tell him.

He's talking now? he asks.

When I place my hand on his head, he speaks less wildly, I say. This is what I have learnt.

He fell ill. He woke up. His brother was gone. He tried to keep going after him. And you found him in the garden.

I don't know what to do, my husband says.

We care for the boy you did find, I say. There is no more.

Did they walk along the riverbed? he asks.

There is mud on his shoes and his clothes. There is nothing else like river mud.

All this way?

The walls thrum slightly as the helicopter passes again, carrying away containers from the abandoned shipping yard. Like a hornet carrying a grub.

They are built out of energy, children, I say. Even when they are ill. They are mainly no more than energy.

Perhaps if I follow the riverbed, he says.

We are not near the riverbed. And you found him here.

But maybe. If I just.

He is that type of man.

I do not tell my husband how I strip the bedclothes from the child and sponge away his sweat. And look at every inch of his skin. How my heart races and I feel sick, certain I will find some sign that he has brought some illness from the city, as there are always whispers of. And then that will be that.

~

As he sips the bowl I hold, pecking like a bird, we have a sort of conversation. Distant though he is, I think he understands.

A robin sings outside the window.

What will your brother do, I ask, when he finds his dog?

Go back to the city.

And if he does not find it? Would he go back anyway?

He won't stop looking for the dog.

He wouldn't stop.

He won't stop looking for his dog.

He wouldn't stop. He wouldn't stop.

~

In the night, the boy gets worse again.

When the Water Train goes by, a shudder rattles through him. As if the train itself races through his body. A sound felt in the darkness through the air.

It makes me shudder, too, to see him.

I think the train wrenches part of him away. If I believed in souls.

~

But in the morning the boy is sitting up.

I have to go, he says. I have to find my brother.

I cannot help believing the train took away the worst of it. The illness. Dragged it, with that shudder, from his body.

Now there is a thin shake through him, as if he is animated by a faint breeze.

I have to go. My brother. He begins to open and close his fists, and I feel uneasy that I knew this was a thing that he would do.

You cannot now. I try to make him calm.

He is eight, he says. I have to look for him.

He has to look for him, before he can look after him.

I must look after him.

When I ask him what age he is himself, he lies and says he's twelve.

He went after his dog.

I know. First you must get strong.

That dog.

My husband will bring courgettes, and beans and greens, and spinach.

He does not look as if he understands what these things are.

You cannot find your brother unless you are strong.

He seems, almost imperceptibly, to nod.

~

Look! my husband says. He holds up a nasturtium leaf and peers at me through a hole right in its centre. Caterpillars, he says with pride.

I do not understand him sometimes.

~

That night the boy goes.

He is barely able to walk, I'm sure.

He climbs out of the window.

He takes a pile of my husband's dirty gardening clothes from the drywash basket.

We find out in the morning.

No, I say, when my husband says he must go after him, fearing that he will have gone towards the train.

He's weak, I think. He's weak.

He had nothing but potato water.

Look after your garden.

I imagine a trail. A dog, a boy, another boy, a man. My man going missing. Then me, I follow after him. My daughter finds me gone. Her partner looks for her. So on. And so on. One by one. A fairy tale. Until we all walk, all of us, one by one away.

LETTER

John,

Where to start?

– Are you sure you're happy to do this?

I could just record something, I know. But then I'd just ramble. You know me. And I want to get it right.

I've asked Ruth to write things down as I speak. Strange, talking into the air. Hearing her voice in my earpiece.

– It's Ruth, right? Thank you, Ruth. Sorry. I knew that. Let's start again.

I've tried to memorise what I want to tell you, but I was never very good at that. The words seem very solid until I go to say them, then they disappear. Like trying to remember my dreams, when I wake up.

Yours always hang with you through the day, you say. I think mine move to make way for daydreams.

- No. Sorry. There's no need for any of that, is there? Try again.

You said, I don't want there to be time, to think of you in pain. Well, I feel the same.

So I've asked them not to tell you. When it's time.

If they told you to come, then you would know.

You would know from the moment they called. And you would know as you were on your way here. And when you got here you would sit here watching. And I would have to think of you going through that.

By the time you got here, I would be asleep. They've said I would be asleep. By then.

So.

- That's right, isn't it? I'll be. By that time.

And I would be asleep, they've said, by then. So.

You would watch. That's all. I would not be able to help.

But this will help, I hope. I want to say some things.

I want to say that I knew in the first few minutes I was going to love you, and would love you, and would fight through things for that.

There are people together all their lives, and they don't have that. But we do. Even through the fights and niggles, and the things that come. We do.

We were so young. And I had never been so sure and determined about anything before, that I couldn't properly understand.

–   I was twenty. You know I was a nurse, too, Ruth. One year older than him, almost to the week. It's funny. Within moments of us meeting, total strangers, such professionals, our faces were closer together than they came for quite a while after that.

–   He was soaking wet. Sodden. Covered in wet earth. And everybody else so clean and bright. They'd

147

bombed the city water pipe, and he was out there. He smelled of mud. Even through the stinky antiseptic. I probably even said, you smell of mud.

– He only looked at me properly once, very quickly, very fully. And I knew.

– Have you had that, Ruth? Have you felt that, ever? Well. Hold out for it . . . I shouldn't say that to you. But. If it ever comes to something like this, for you, it will matter. That you're with the right one.

– Sorry. I said. I chatter. Okay. Say,

You told me once that you'd rather I die first.

I was angry when you said it. But.

I understand it now. I understand.

It wasn't so I didn't have to go through losing you. But so you didn't have to watch me being brave. And know about the awful thing of me carrying on bravely.

– We see it, don't we? Us nurses. The carrying on.

- She told him, didn't she? Doctor Sandhu.

- Thank you. I know you're not meant to say.

- I could see. When they spoke this morning. They looked so strange, watery, through this pod. Just dim shapes. But I know. He would have held his eyes open too wide; he would have stroked the scar on his jaw.

- That's funny, isn't it? That thing. That the first time I touched him was to pull that scar together. That it could have been another nurse. But it was me.

- I stitched a thread to him, he says. And him there, I could tell, just thinking. Over what had happened, the men they hadn't managed to save. They'd gone back and forth, pulling them out of the water that was spilling out of the pipe. It was sort of still going on in his eyes.

- We joke I sewed in some sort of secret communication device. Not just the thread he jokes about. He says, when I feel the smooth skin there, run my finger on the scar, I can hear you tell me things.

- You must have silly things like that. With. Are you with someone?

- Colin. You must have silly things with Colin.

- Sorry. I didn't mean to say you *didn't* have the right thing with him. Earlier. I'm a bit. Sorry. Chattering. Could you read out what I've said.

- Yes,

So you didn't have to watch me being brave.

- Write,

I understand that now.

I know you hate the idea of me being in pain, but I am not. They've seen to that.

Actually, I've had fun. Daydreamer, me. And you have too.

I've turned my bed, the bubble of the pod, into all sorts.

Been places with you, these last few weeks, you wouldn't quite believe.

We've dived together in a submarine. We saw extraordinary fish.

We went through space. We landed on a star. A bright, bright rock.

You sat beside me on a sled that magic animals pulled across the city sky.

It's a four-poster bed in a castle room. You stacked your armour in the corner.

It's a raft on a wide, open river.

An expedition tent. Us dressed intrepidly, Victorians.

It's easy to imagine.

All the paper flowers you've brought. On the windowsill, the extra bedside cabinet. At a certain time of evening, as the light slants in, they throw shadows on the walls, like giant jungle plants.

I hope that makes you smile.

And that's the thing I suppose I want to say the most.

Smile.

I'm torn up between the joy of knowing you will keep on living, and the fear my dying will ruin it all for you. The world.

But you're going to have to love it for us both. That's an order.

The smell of stone in the air when it rains after days of sun. There's a word for that. Petrichor.

Seeing a broken umbrella in a bin. Knowing someone has given up and let themselves embrace the downpour.

Smile at them.

There will be a time when you find yourself laughing, and feel guilty. Do not.

That you will suddenly realise you have not thought of me for hours, and feel angry with yourself. Do not.

You know I've always needed time to myself. So sometimes I'll be off somewhere. But not gone.

I know . . .

–   Sorry. Ruth. Are you? You look a little.

–   You're sure?

–   Okay. Then,

I know, when I die, it will be another ordinary day.

There will be no great war. No great global disaster. No buildings will collapse. No bombs will fall. No forests will burn.

I'll just be gone.

When I do. When I am. I know that what you'll miss the most is talking.

Don't let it stop.

You know me, and you know what I'd say.

And there's the scar, of course, in case. No beard. Promise me that. Don't hide it.

Once I can't be there to stop you.

You are out there now, as I write this. Say this.

  – Put. No, put as Ruth writes this down for me.
    Would you mind?

And that you'll be hearing my voice.

You'll be having conversations with me in your head.
You've told me that you do. That you hear my voice.

Well. I'm not really there, am I, right now?

So, there shouldn't be a difference. When the arms and
legs and nose bits of me's gone.

I know you. You will keep everything all bunched inside
your head fighting one another and it will all go roaring
around.

But do not let that drown me out.

The smell of me will fade.

The feel of me will fade.

That's okay.

But do not let my voice go, John.

Make that your duty, now.

Keep my voice alive, and hear me.

That way I will live.

I need to know this is not it for me, and that we can still talk.

People do not talk. And they get themselves in awful trouble.

Don't let this be the end of.

- Sorry, Ruth. I'm. This is. Ruth? I didn't mean to . . . You're upset. I'm sorry. I shouldn't be asking you to do this.

- I know. But. Even so. We can't help it, can we? We're born to care. How would we be able to do the job we do, did, unless we were unable not to? I bet you collected snails, when you were little, and looked after them in a little box. You did. I knew. I did too. Banded snails. They were quite unusual. I used to collect them when we visited the beach, from the sharp grass of the sand dunes. I'd look after them all day. Not interested in sandcastles. Good. I've made you smile at least, as well as cry.

- Some people, a lot of people, are just born to be a certain thing. John was born to duty. That's his compass point.

- I knew when I asked him, when we first met, 'please don't be a soldier', there was no point asking him to be a gardener instead.

- What does he do? Your. Colin. Journalist. He should write this. It's terrible, isn't it? I wish I could write. When it comes to it how we can't really say what we mean. A hug would be much easier.

- It must be nice, to be with someone who can use their words properly.

- We didn't hug enough. I think we would have hugged more as we got old together.

- Sorry. My mouth is so dry.

- Are you happy with Colin? Sorry. I shouldn't ask. But you don't . . .

- Don't wait, Ruth. Don't wait to find out.

- Doctor? Oh. Yes. Of course.

- Now?

- Of course. Do I have a moment?

- Okay.

- Just. Yes, of course. Could I have just a moment, please.

- Get rid of everything I've said. I guess.

- Just. Thank you, Ruth.

- Could you write.

John,

I know what you'll miss the most is talking.

But here I am.

You can hear my voice, right?

Kiss.

PATROL

The pocked footings of the old pipeline stood along the route of the track, damaged some, and split, thundered by the defence guns of the train.

Rust bled about the bleak white concrete from the reinforcing steel.

The rain thudded. Made a cave for Branner's mind.

The dream he'd had, night after night now, played across the inside of Branner's vision. Sat like a sheet of picture glass he had to peer through at the world.

The doctor's words thumped against it over and over.

The dawn intensified, a brightness in the heavy rain.

I do not want there to be time, to think of you in pain.

He'd arrived last night, from the city, for the first light shift.

'Go,' she'd said. 'I understand.'

Branner saw the red dot flash on the grid scanner in his hand; at the same time heard his earpiece hiss. It brought him round.

'I've seen it,' Branner said into his mic.

The sergeant's voice came through the earpiece, through the snap of rain on Branner's hood. The red dot shifting on the scanner. A slight condensation come to the edges of the screen.

'Can you get there?' the sergeant asked.

'I can get there,' Branner answered. He was pushed in against the willow fifty metres from the track. Whatever had set the scanner off was close.

'Let the train guns take it,' said the sergeant.

'No. I'll go,' said Branner. He felt the old scar catch against the nap inside his hood.

160

'I made it look like a train track,' his wife would joke. Appropriate, now, somehow.

It will be an animal, Branner thought.

The rain drummed. Drummed against the doctor's words, the dream. Gathered and fell heavy from the long leaves of willow.

Why let the automatic train guns fire pointlessly?

Branner checked his rifle and walked towards the track.

~

'Are you sure about this, John?' the superintendent had asked. 'You know you can take leave.'

'I'd rather work,' Branner assured him.

'Yesterday, on the rooftop . . .' Concerns about Branner had been raised. The way he had shown doubt.

'I'm fine, sir,' Branner said.

The superintendent had to make a judgement.

'Do you know? Have they?' the superintendent faltered.

'No, sir. They can't be sure how long.'

Branner had sensed the superintendent wanted to ask, 'Would it not be more difficult to be so far from her? Would staying in the city not be better?' But the superintendent did not ask this.

'You were on the line as a young lad in the army, is that right? When it was the pipe,' is what he'd asked. 'Before you joined the police. The youngest ever to be decorated.'

Branner simply nodded.

Perhaps that was why he wanted to be out here. To go back to the beginning, so he did not see the end.

~

Steam still came from the damp earth.

There were six of them, he the youngest, barely old enough to leave the base, sitting on logs around the covered pit.

The timber squad had not been through here yet, and they had to work around the downed trunks as they cut and burned the brash, their job to make a barren margin along the line so anyone who attempted to approach the pipe could more easily be seen.

It was midsummer. Bright light bounced off the pipeline's flank. The thick rain had passed an hour ago. They took a break for lunch.

The spade went sharply into the soil with the sound of a hatchet into green wood.

As they dug a little deeper the soil got drier, and didn't give that sound, and seemed, in drying out, to lose its earthy smell.

He was setting up a place to cut the muntjac up but turned at the noise the others made when they got to the charred grasses they'd packed around the meat.

Moments later the smell of the cooked deer reached him, and the feeling was so intense and primitive he wanted it to persist. Wished bizarrely that he had to wait a little longer.

The corporal picked the deer up with the spade because it was cooked so well it simply fell apart.

He put it on the makeshift table and they ate it with their fingers. A chunk of ration bread in one hand, and the other hand alternately lifting their canteens of clearwater and picking at the meat.

Look, said one of the men, fishing a partially flattened bullet from the muntjac's flesh. I would have thought it would have gone straight through.

It was then the first device went off.

The first they knew of it was a ripple in the ground. He saw the bones they'd cast about - that they'd slid cleanly from the meat - bounce somehow, as if they had suddenly decided to reanimate. Then there was the sound of the explosion.

~

There were four teams in the area at the time, all within a click. The device had sundered the pipe exactly at the point where one of the teams were resting.

When they got there, the bodies of the team already looked long dead because the water that sluiced about them cleaned them of blood and bloated their skin. They knew some were alive only because of the noise they made, swallowed in the deafening crash of still-coming water.

The great wings of steel that had been blasted into the ground around the pipe hissed with heat. Brought steam up from the wet soil. Spat in the gathering water.

The earth rippled again, and he saw circles form on the surface of a shallow pool. Instinctively hit the ground.

Then the second bomb went off. Like a building crashing down.

Those that were not dead but badly injured began drowning in the water. Three of them still stood. Amongst them, him.

He was confused as to why his chest was slick with blood until he realised it was his own and felt sick as he acknowledged the flap of skin hanging at his jaw. But it was superficial.

His head spun. He looked up at a lifted patch of bank beyond the pipe that seemed almost liquid itself in the sun and his only thought was to go to it and sit. Then his corporal's shout reset him.

The water came endlessly as they dragged the bodies from the pools. They were barely able to hear themselves. The corporal screamed into the comms to cut the flow. But even if they had, the bombs were timed to detonate as far as possible from the stop-gate.

When eventually the water died it did so suddenly. Lost ferocity; and the roar of it ebbed. From the white hissing force, it turned at the same time rich and brittle, a smooth ribbon dropping from the torn mouth of the pipe.

And as it slowed, they heard the rattle.

A clatter coming closer. Clanging and echoing in the emptied pipe.

Then silence. Relatively.

The tap of spilled water losing urgency. The breath of the men.

A clear metallic ping as whatever travelled their way came to rest at a section junction of the pipe.

What were they to do?

The tap now, of the dripping water, tap tap, like a timer.

There were still men in the water.

The pools that formed were dark with soil and thick with leaves and debris.

They left the shrapnel in the wounds. Where the bones had slipped effortlessly from the muntjac's meat, the iron had seared itself into the soldiers' flesh.

Behind closed doors they felt the sharp end of Command's reprimand for disobeying orders. They'd been ordered to retreat.

Publicly, they were given medals.

Six had died. Two drowned, and four died of their wounds.

Everyone else they saved.

It would have killed them too, the third device, had it not malfunctioned.

She talked about this as she stitched him up, her eyes filled with concentration. And, 'You're my first,' she said. He had to force himself to look away from her. To look at anything but her.

Never the obvious things that caused the shell around the memory to crack. Not the cordite smell of the firing range. The cool metallic echo of the transport vehicles. Nor even the surgical cleanliness of her ward.

Just this time, on a rooftop, the wing of a bird.

For a split second the falcon had sharply gleamed; then was a dark object hurtling for a brief eternity away. And the compressed roar. The discreet detonation somewhere deep within the pipe.

A quiet force he'd felt loudly in the centre of his body.

The shrapnel winging through the sky.

When he heard the couple in the penthouse through their open window, he felt himself drop through the building. All the lives in the storeys below him.

Felt the memory, out there at the pipeline, that he hoped would blur the dream, the thoughts of her, begin to break up, then the doctor's words blow it once more to fragments.

The deep river of the crowd marching below.

Felt suddenly the building itself would sunder.

That only he held it safe.

And he wanted to jump. To step off its edge.

Did not. Because, as now, he feared there would be no ground to hit.

Could think only of the rush of the air.

~

And the shudder, that comes into the rails, brings all this back to Branner. As they make before thunder, the pheasant call. Before that first detonation. His face, an image pitted in the reflection off the solar sleeper as he puts his hand out to the track.

The drumming of the heavy rain. Hits his hood. Hits hood. Pools beside the track in the shallows in the ground. Runs amongst the rails and clinker, bubbling into welts. Urgent ruptures in the bank.

The water bright as molten metal.

The great machines that worked along the route to cut and smelt the pipe. To re-cast the iron as rails.

To change its purpose from a structure of containment, to instruments of guidance.

How her hand tightened. His grip tensing on the scanner, grown slippery with wet.

The distraught footings; how the light had bounced that day.

'You need to speed it up, John.' Sergeant through the comms.

Counts his steps between them. Uses them, to help himself proceed. A mechanism of duty. Help himself go on.

Hit hood. Pit pat. Focus on the dot.

What of the train, and everything it is, if the track is ripped away?

Wet metal smell and stone.

The dryness up on that rooftop, the heat reflected as if it came up off the stones.

Those first weeks, together. Lying on the beach. 'Join the police,' she'd asked him. 'Please don't be a soldier.'

Smell of earth now. Kicked-up leaves. A plump grub displaced from the leaf litter as Branner skids down from the track. A grotesque. Visitation.

Focus, Branner, focus.

The insects hung in ghosts above the line.

Stop thinking of her face.

As if from space, the sergeant's voice, 'Can you make this?' through the bubble.

Yes. He says he can.

'Just leave it, Branner. Stay clear. It'll be another dog.'

The rain hits with the rhythm of train wheels. Hits hood. Hit his hood. Pushes Branner into his brain. His scar catching faintly on the soft pile of the coat with every movement of his head.

You asked. You made this happen. By preferring she died first.

The long-downed brash at the edge of the track tangled now in new-come growth. Rain steaming on the warmer soil.

You could let the train pass. Switch off your greenlighter, become unrecognisable, and let the train defences fire.

Would you even feel the guns?

The shudder now comes to the ground, as if it were a sound, shakes Branner's mind minutely; rattles, his mind inside its hood, clattering, the rain.

'Take the shot,' the sergeant orders, bluntly in the comms.

If you die first, then she can die in peace.

A great noise. Then you would be gone.

Reaching now, to try to hear. To ask her what to do.

The red dot on the darkening undergrowth in the mid-scope of his rifle, the rain a veil sheeting off his hood.

How a glow comes through the opaque pod around her bed. As if she is a source of light.

'Branner.' Urgent now, the sergeant's voice.

Just switch off your greenlighter. That's all it would take.

The air seeming to shatter ahead of the oncoming force.

Dry mouth. Possibility. Brief Armageddon of the guns.

A tensile sing come to the rails.

But. Without you she is gone.

Hit. Hood. The rain. The train. Pools gathered round him where he's knelt to take the shot. Ten million gallons of water, two hundred miles an hour.

'. . . seconds,' lost in thickening noise. The bullet's path, a dream burst into flame and char. The train some crashing wave.

The rifle calculates for distance, calculates for force.

The old scar tacks against the soft nap of his hood.

Tell me.

Tell me, Anne.

They should not be here. In this place. Deer, dog, or man.

Pull the trigger, John.

Stay living.

Keep my voice alive.

AUTHOR'S NOTE

The world of *Stillicide* had been in my mind for a long time. I always felt it would find form as a set of short narratives that would pool together to tell a wider story. When Di Speirs asked whether I had an idea for twelve interconnected radio pieces, it was a fit.

Stories had to stand alone but present a greater whole, and each had to run fifteen minutes read out in an early-evening Sunday slot.

The stories in the book differ only slightly from those first heard during the summer, 2019.

ACKNOWLEDGEMENTS

Thanks to David Goddard of the British Dragonfly Society. Scarce Chasers first emerge in May, and the manuscript had to be ready before this. He went into his attic and found me an exuvia.

Thanks, of course, to Di Speirs for inviting me to write these stories; to producer Justine Willett; and to Laura Barber and the team at Granta.

Thanks to the actors who read these pieces for BBC Radio 4 in the summer of 2019 – Richard Goulding; Stephen Campbell Moore; Hattie Morahan; Philip Arditti; John Bowler; Alex Jennings; Katherine Press; James Cosmo; Lydia Wilson; Sudha Bhuchar; Richard Woska; and Anne-Marie Duff.

Thanks also to Josh Uddin for taking me up to the roof, for the view from the 43rd floor. To Euan and all at A.M. Heath, and to Chris de Jong; and to you two, who help me know the future will not be a bleak place.

Also by Cynan Jones and available from Granta Books
www.granta.com

THE LONG DRY

WINNER OF A BETTY TRASK AWARD

'Lovely, poignant . . . and resonant' Sarah Waters

When the farmer wakes at dawn, he can already feel the heat of the day rising and the silence from his wife hanging heavy in the air. As he sets out across his parched fields to find a missing cow, his mind starts to turn over the dreams he harbours, the cares he and his wife both carry alone, and the uneasy sense that something is about to change. Written with clarity and depth, this is a powerful novel about the fragility of life and the small, unseen moments upon which fate twists.

'The best book I've read this year' Andrew Davies

'A paean to the corruptibility of the flesh . . . characterised by moments of startling imagery and stirringly intense lyrical beauty. A wee, wonderful book' Niall Griffiths

'A convincing glimpse of life in all its beauty and sadness' *Big Issue*

'From first to last, through spare style, human empathy, and wonderfully observed detail, Jones attains a pitch of emotional involvement that is mesmerising. The effect is beautiful' Tim Pears

EVERYTHING I FOUND ON THE BEACH

'An excellent novel. Beautiful and haunting . . . [it] will make your heart race' *Time Out* ★★★★

Take three strangers who all want something more. The Polish shift worker struggling to get a foothold in the new country; a fisherman who needs to make good on a promise to his best friend; and the middle man, determined to make up for lost time and take a little of what he deserves. When a chance comes along, each man must weigh the risk – and then keep his nerve as events take on their own unstoppable momentum. Tightly plotted and sharply observed, this is a gripping story of desperation and duty, and the brutal struggle to progress.

'A compelling novel that confirms Jones as a thrilling new presence' *Western Mail*

'Is Jones as good a writer as they say? Without a doubt. Edgy, elegant prose combined with masterful characterization and plot, this novel is everything I had hoped for, and more. Read it, then read it again' R. J. Ellory

Also by Cynan Jones and available from Granta Books
www.granta.com

THE DIG

WINNER OF A JERWOOD FICTION UNCOVERED
AWARD 2014

'Profound, powerful and utterly absorbing' *Guardian*

'A brilliant novel – tense, tough and haunting' Joe Dunthorne

Deep in rural Wales, a farmer is struggling through lambing season
when he becomes aware that his land is being stalked by a badger-
baiter who brings with him the stark threat of violence. Built of
the interlocking fates of these two solitary men, this is a searing
story of isolation and loss, from a writer of uncommon gifts.

'Stellar . . . There is no doubt that Jones is one of the most
talented writers in Britain' *Independent on Sunday*

'*The Dig* is deeply moving . . . It is a book about the essentials:
life and death, cruelty and compassion. It is a book that will get
in your bones, and haunt you' *Daily Telegraph*

'A marvellous novel . . . There are echoes of Ted Hughes,
Cormac McCarthy, Ernest Hemingway . . . It can be read like
poetry, letting the words resonate in the skull' *The Times*

'Written with a beautifully blunt simplicity, *The Dig* is moving,
evocative, and utterly compelling' Jon McGregor

Also by Cynan Jones and available from Granta Books
www.granta.com

COVE

SHORTLISTED FOR THE WALES BOOK OF THE YEAR FICTION PRIZE

A short story drawn from this novel, published in the *New Yorker* as 'The Edge of the Shoal', won the BBC National Short Story Award 2017.

'A masterclass . . . writing stripped back to the bone, and storytelling that gets under the skin. Powerful and terrifying'
Jon McGregor

Out at sea, in a sudden storm, a man is struck by lightning. When he wakes, injured and adrift, he must fight to piece things back together. Who he is; where he is; and, overriding everything, how he will return to the woman he dimly senses waits for his return.

'A haunting meditation on trauma and human fragility'
Financial Times

'Hypnotically compelling . . . A terrific read' Colin Barrett

'Stark and elemental' *Metro*

'Lyrical . . . and intense' *Sunday Telegraph*